'Steeped in Julian of Norwich's *Revelations of Divine Love*, and based on careful historical research, this fictional recreation of Julian's life is both gripping and profoundly believable.'

Santha Bhattacharji, University of Oxford

'Dreamy. Am tempted to become a mystic myself.'

Julian Clary

'This is a rich and intriguing book, which is profoundly thought-provoking and helps the reader to get to know Julian in an entirely new way.'

Paula Gooder

'I was completely hooked and considerably moved by the life and thoughts of this exceptional woman.'

Jeremy Irons

'Julian of Norwich was a woman for her turbulent times. Through Claire Gilbert's powerful telling, readers in our own turbulent times can encounter Julian and be assured that all will ultimately "be well".'

Sister Jane Livesey CJ

'*I, Julian* is a tour de force, a rich re-imagining of the life of Julian of Norwich and a disturbing evocation of the life of the merchant class in Norwich in the fourteenth century.'

Julia Neuberger

'What a wonderful book! It is as if we have finally found the lost autobiography of one of the medieval world's most important women. Julian's voice rings out true on every page and a deep understanding of her world and her work underpins each line. It is a joy to read.'

Janina Ramirez

'Claire Gilbert inhabits Julian of Norwich in the way that Hilary Mantel immersed herself in Cromwell. This is living fiction.'

Sarah Sands

'A life and a time so convincingly summoned that it's hard to believe this is a work of fiction, proof that the imagination can be just as true as the truth.'

Frances Stonor Saunders

'Claire Gilbert has miraculously stepped inside the body and soul of Julian of Norwich, through her extraordinary life. Its method strongly reminded me of Maggie O'Farrell's *Hamnet*.'

Rt Hon Jack Straw

'I enjoyed and admired *I, Julian* very much. It is extraordinarily deft and sensitive. This book is going to introduce many new readers to Julian and inspire others who know her slightly to go back with fresh eyes and a re-invigorated sense of how her writing developed and in what sort of historical setting. It really is a striking book, and an impressive achievement.'

Nicholas Watson, Harvard University

'Written with profound insight, spiritual and psychological, and a rare sensitivity to the everyday world of the fourteenth century, *I, Julian* is a brilliantly illuminating companion to one of the greatest works of spiritual writing in English.'

Rowan Williams

'It is a beautiful, intensely moving achievement which not only excites literary admiration: it renews the reader's faith that "all shall be well".'

A. N. Wilson

I, JULIAN

CLAIRE GILBERT

HODDER &
STOUGHTON

First published in Great Britain in 2023 by Hodder & Stoughton
An Hachette UK company

5

A CIP catalogue record for this title is available from the British Library

Hardback ISBN 978 1 399 80752 4
eBook ISBN 978 1 399 80753 1

Typeset in Adobe Garamond by Hewer Text UK Ltd, Edinburgh
Printed and bound in Great Britain by Clays Ltd, Elcograf S.p.A.

Hodder & Stoughton policy is to use papers that are natural, renewable
and recyclable products and made from wood grown in sustainable
forests. The logging and manufacturing processes are expected to
conform to the environmental regulations of the country of origin.

Hodder & Stoughton Ltd
Carmelite House
50 Victoria Embankment
London EC4Y 0DZ

www.hodderfaith.com

For Seán, always
and Father Eamonn, who did not laugh when I said I raved

What follows is a work of the imagination

1403

PROLOGUE

What would my life have been if you had laughed with the others when I said I raved, Thomas?

I would not be here in this anchorhold and I would not have written a word.

In the silence where your laughter was not, the visions were real again. And all that my life became flowed from that moment. Because my return to the fierce light of my meeting with Jesu banished everything else. There would be no second husband, no household to manage, no busy works of charity. I could not do those things again and attend to the visions, and if the visions were true, I had to choose them. And then I had to receive all that they showed me, more and more seeing, till the words to understand what I was seeing filled my heart and overflowed and I had to start writing them down. And I understood that these words I was writing were not for me but so that others could see for themselves what I had seen.

It was not safe to write. Not in English, not these dangerous words and especially not as a woman. I had to trust that if I wrote the words, and they could be kept in secret, they would be read one day.

Some think that to enter an anchorhold is to choose death. They are right, it is a kind of death, and one I welcomed. I knew death: I had walked towards its pain and loss and I had tasted the joy that is the other side of the pain. So it was not a hard choice for me. Here was safety; here I could take time, years and more years, to reflect on what I had seen and let it grow in me and write it down privily. I was alone and undisturbed; I did not need to guard my words, my dangerous truth, my woman's truth.

And now I have finished the writing, and the words have been taken away from this place by hands that I trust, to wait until they can be read. The danger is passed from me.

What is left, Thomas?

An old woman on tired knees. Aside from prayer, my work is done.

But here you are at my window, asking for more words. Not of the visions, but of my life. Mine!

You say that when this long account of my visions finally comes to be read, perhaps many years from now, people will want to know who I am and they will want to know about my life, because they will see me as their teacher. You whisper that I am a great teacher already. You are wrong. I am not a teacher and I do not want those who read my words to see me.

But oh, Thomas, I owe you my life. This life, this rich, anchored life. And I do have more words in me. And yes, they are of myself. They come in answer to a question that has never been far from me. A question that stays strong even as my body grows weaker, as it draws close to death once again and this time with neither hope nor wish to return.

Why?

Why did these showings come to me, wretch that I am? Why?

You believed me when I did not believe myself, Thomas, and I will tell you my life, and you perhaps will hear the answer to my question if I cannot. I will speak truly. But I will speak privately, for I will not have you make my life more important than the words I have written which have gone from here.

I do not want my story broadcast, Thomas.

I

Yes. I will tell you: your face is soft, you do not judge me, you never have, seated here at my window, comfortable and big-bellied and unalarming, inhabiting your black Benedictine robes with humility not pride, following my words with nods or smiles or even tears, as you did all those years ago when you first came to me, as you have always done.

The words are coming, and the memories.

1347–1350

II

I see again the child that I was, intense, active, impatiently pushing my fine, always-tangled, mousy-brown hair out of my eyes, full of questions, lonely. I was rarely with other children, for I was my parents' only child and we lived quietly outside the city in a small-holding, with Marion our maid and my nurse in strict and stiff-boned attendance. Yes, I was intense, and sensitive. I felt everything too much, like a soft cobnut without its shell, easily startled into tears by a lonely, hungry tramp; the ewe-mother of a stillborn lamb; even a flower broken at its stem by a thoughtless human hand.

I saw these things, noticed them on my long solitary wandering through the woods and fields by our home, because my parents always asked me what I had seen that day, when dusk gathered us inside and around the hearth. I on my stool, speaking of my seeing, my mother spinning and smiling at my words, Marion mercifully elsewhere, my father massive in his chair in the flickering shadows, returned from his wool merchanting in the city, protection and his presence one and the same to me.

The best time is in the summer, for it is still light when I finish my reporting and my father stands up and says,

Time for our chores, daughter.

And I jump up from my stool and run after him as he strides to the door and outside, and there he takes my upstretched hands and swings me onto his shoulders, and together we inspect the small-holding, ensuring the fencing is secure and the three sheep and the two goats are safely within and have water, and the horse in his stall has water and hay, and we make sure the hens are all gathered in their run and that they have water, then we go to the fruit trees and see how the apples are ripening, and we walk up and down the rows of vegetables and comment on their growth, kneeling from time to time to remove a weed. I am in heights of happiness riding so tall on my father's shoulders, queen of all I survey, holding tightly to his ears or if he complains at my pulling burying my hands in the thick thatch of his black hair, then clutching tightly around his neck as he bends and straightens at the fencing or the weeds, laughing with delight at the sudden swooping danger, knowing I am safe, that I will always be safe because my father is here.

And suddenly, he is not here.

III

It is the first pestilence. We do not know what is happening to us, nothing like this has been seen before. There is always sickness and death but now a new, ugly, pitiless, mortal sickness moves among us more swiftly than thought or prayer. We do not know where it comes from; we walk in fear of an enemy we cannot see but know is all around, that will strike silently from any side including from within. You fear your neighbour, even your own kin, you fear the food set before you to eat, the ale that you drink, the water in which you bathe, the air you breathe, the very clothes on your back.

I am only seven and I feel the fear not in these details but in those who protect me, my mother and my father. If they are afraid then I am not safe.

They are afraid.

And today as I stand at the gate of our cottage to greet my father riding back from the city, even from a distance I can see he is not well. He draws near, his whole body is gathered to itself in pain, and moans spill from his lips at every movement of his horse. He does not see me and nor does my mother as she comes running from the cottage to help him dismount and stumble inside. His smell as they pass makes me want to be sick. Rotting flesh.

He is brought to his bedchamber, and our home in the days that follow is like a body clenched, locked in tension, holding its breath. I escape as much as I can, out into the woods that surround our cottage, down to the river where it flows beyond the city. I am not heeded; I stay away for hours each day, trying to pretend to myself that all is well at home, trying to lose myself in the detail of my lonely walks as I always did before. I look at a sycamore leaf brown and curled on the path, placed so delicately, its edge hardly touching the earth, prey to the wind and to the crushing footfall of men. I look at a bright-eyed sparrow on a tree-twig twitch its tail before flying away from me, dipping between branches. I look at the scales of a fish dead on the jetty catch the sun and flash rainbow colours, each scale distinct and shining. And all the time I remember that I cannot return and tell my father what I have seen, because he is abed and dying.

The sun is warm and I go to the river where they say the pestilence does not linger. I lie on my front on the bank and watch plop-ripples make circles on the surface of the water, like rain but they come from underneath, from water boatmen as they reach up to catch their insect prey and then retreat. I make a palm-sized world with my hands cupped either side of my eyes, a world with no dying father, no distracted, white-faced mother, no waspish Marion. Into my private world, my safe world which I make with my cupped hands, floats my very own water boatman, hanging just below the surface of the water, his wing-oars outstretched and gently moving to keep him still and buoyant, like men would in a boat, but he is breathing underwater as they could not. I see my palm-sized world through his eyes: full of dark green and light green fronds of waterweed, huge to him. He has a scaly body, his antennae twitch, he is a fish-insect, and suddenly he shoots faster than my sluggish human eyes can follow, out of my palm-sized world, to his prey I think: it is not a safe world for them. The longer I am still the more I see, more and more movement of creatures from dots and specks of flies to stately fish, moving through my palm-sized world. I gently dip my finger into the water, slowly so that it does not disturb, and watch the creatures as their fear abates and they approach and nuzzle or swim around this great clumsy pacific intruder.

When reluctantly I return, Marion is standing in the doorway. She looks thunderous.

> You neglect your father, she says. You should be near him and pray for him. Do you not love him? That is what he thinks. He thinks that you do not care.

I draw in my breath, wincing at Marion's accusing finger and her admonition. Guilt breaks open in me and floods my heart. My father thinks I do not love him? Squirming away from Marion's hand as it pushes me unkindly through the cottage to his bedchamber, scared of what I will see but driven by Marion and my guilt, I go to the stinking place where he has lain for days. I land splat, hard on my knees, outside the door, pushed by Marion.

> It is not safe to enter, she hisses, but you can stay here and pray – pray loudly so he can hear you.

I am terrified.

Where is my mother?

Not here.

With no further explanation, Marion opens the chamber door wide, looking at my face with vindictive satisfaction as she passes by me and away.

I can see him.

This is not my father.

> *Pater noster,*
> Our Father, I cry out in the Latin I have learned, *qui es in caelis,*
> who art in heaven
> Hallowed be thy name

A shrunken distorted frame lies abed, stick-like arms and legs held stiffly akimbo, claw hands curled over a belly as round and distended as though it were bearing a child.

> Thy kingdom come

I can see stains on the bedclothes draped over lumpen swellings where the arms and legs begin, and above the blankets the neck bulges with bulbous egg-shaped lumps, some oozing foul-smelling muck, holding the head in stiff stillness.

> Thy will be done

The face has paper-thin skin patched purple, drawn over jutting cheekbones, teeth bared, moaning breaths, eyes staring upwards.

In earth as it is in heaven

It *is* my father's face.

Give us this day our daily bread
And forgive us our trespasses

It *is* my father and he is here, lost in this rotting, stiffly held frame;
he is not elsewhere, ready to protect me, filling his chair by the fire
and the whole room with his great black-haired black-eyed comforting healthy presence, laughing at my stories of what I have seen that
day.

As we . . . my voice falters . . . as we forgive those

He is here, helpless. He is here and he does not know me. My strong
father, helpless and in so much pain. And there is nothing I can do
for him.

Except pray. I make myself stay kneeling repeating the *Pater
Noster* over and over again, watching in fascinated horror the restless movements and moans until they become more pronounced,
moans drowning my stumbling words, the head is moving from
side to side on the pillow and now the lips smack horribly over
the large yellowed teeth, and the tongue, a rasping dry thing,
pokes out of the mouth, and he cries out words I cannot discern
and I do not know what he means or what he needs. I only know
he is in terrible pain and needs help and I do not know what to
do and I am alone with him, where is Marion, where is my
mother? I can bear it no longer and I start up from my knees just
as my mother appears with a bowl and I push past her and run

out of the cottage out into the woods down to the river and throw myself on the bank and weep more tears than all the deep flowing river can possibly hold, flowing past me, flowing onwards, onwards to the sea.

IV

The next day the moans from the bedchamber abate and the house is no longer so clenched in fear. Our curate appears and is taken to my father, the door of the bedchamber closed behind him. My mother bids me wait with her in the solar, and while we are there she says,

It will not be long before your father is taken from us. He is quiet now, and if you come to him you will see that he is at peace. Will you come? I will be with you and you need not be afraid.

I nod wordlessly. I do not want to return to that room, to that body, but I want to please my mother. And in the hall Marion looks up from her sweeping and her face accuses me and that stirs me too: she does not think I have done enough to prove my love. So I take my mother's hand and return to the bedchamber, kneeling again at the open door while she enters and kneels near the bed.

That was a good thing to do, Thomas. For the body I see is still now, covered in fresh bedclothes, the smell is softened by lavender, his eyes are closed and he looks peaceful. I can see he is at peace and my own heart settles. I watch as he takes a great juddering breath, and lets it out, and then does not breathe in for so long that I think he has died, but then he takes another great breath, and lets it out, and for even longer does not breathe, and again I think he has died, and then another breath . . . The priest speaks prayers and anoints his closed eyes with oil, then his lips, murmuring more words of absolution, and then – and it looks so funny that despite everything laughter spurts up in me, which I hold in with all my might – his nose and his ears, and then his hands and his feet, and my mother turns to me and her eyes are full of tears but she nods and smiles a little and I know he is safe now, shriven and safe.

He dies later that day, just one week from when he fell ill, and his body is taken away by the authorities with the many, many other bodies that have fallen to the pestilence. We may not bury him and mourn him, it is not permitted to do so, says my mother. We must mourn him in our hearts.

But I do not know how to mourn him. I do not know what I should feel. I think I should be glad that his suffering has ended, and he must be in heaven for the priest shrived him. But I am not glad. I do not know what to do with the great empty space in my heart where his love used to be. It does not feel like anything.

I fret. Does that mean I didn't love him? Is Marion right? Is there more I should have done for him? Am I – am I to blame for his death?

What if I don't love my mother enough and she dies too?

My mother's eyes are huge and lost, her hair whitened under her wimple, her once-soft body thin and hard from her own unhappiness, and she barely sees me, I think, when at mealtimes I steal glances at her face and her armpits for signs of illness.

Lost and unhappy though I am, I dare not go to my mother for comfort. It does not occur to me that I can or should. She is gathered to herself, with little enough strength for her own needs, and I believe I must support her by demanding nothing of her, only praying for her and finding my own solace somehow: among the trees, by the river, in myself.

Marion leaves our home as soon as my father dies, taking his horse as parting payment. I am relieved beyond anything. Now, Thomas, I can see that my mother must have been aware of Marion's unkind bullying and sent her away for my sake; she must have been aware of me. But I do not feel it at the time. Silently I bear this emptiness and confusion and fear inside myself, a little child, Thomas, feeling so responsible and so burdened. Uncomforted.

V

The priests tell us that the pestilence is sent by God to punish our sins. God is angry.

We join a procession of penitents, my mother and I, making its way to London, walking in their wake, trying to pray with them, but I feel as though I am drowning in their moaning, weeping, droning cries of *miserere mei Deus*, have mercy on me O God, mercy, mercy, and my eyes are drawn again and again to the violence with which they beat their own backs, even though I am sickened by it, their tunics torn, bare flesh torn and bleeding for mercy, mercy. The men seek to quell God's wrath by forcing blood from their own bodies by their own hands. Is *this* what God wants? Will *this* satisfy Him and make Him withhold His hand, the vengeful hand that visited the pestilence upon us and took my father and might take my mother? I flinch from Him, and from the raw wounds the men make on their bodies to appease Him, and I look up at my mother's face and see the raw pain there not self-inflicted but sent by God, this angry God. He must be so angry, when He is so ready to hurt us Himself. How can I ever appease Him? All I have in my heart is a great gaping emptiness. Should I beat my own back? But I do not think I could do it, and I do not think my mother would let me anyway.

We walk with the penitents for one day. Back at our home, my mother sits on a low stool and draws me to her so my face is at the same level as her face, and she whispers she is sorry to have shown me such things. Her face is anxious as she looks at me but her voice is no longer clogged by tears as she says,

This is not how we should pray. Instead we can go to the cathedral and hear a mass, and there we will repent our failings, whatever they may be, which have brought such sorrow upon us, with the monks who do not beat themselves but never cease their prayer.

She gives a little nod, as if to herself.

*

The cathedral is overwhelming.

I stand with my eyes stretched wide and my mouth open, till my mother shuts it, in a vast space made bigger by the walls, shocked by the bright blaze of colour, brighter than any I have seen in nature, a motley of blue and green and red and sharp gold in shapes covering the painted walls, glowing glass flashing from the windows and the carved wood and the polished stone and marble mosaic floor, a swirling burst of colours overflowing my eyes and I see only a blur of coloured light; I look up and up till my eyes reach the ceiling higher than any canopy in the green forest, dizzy in this painted stone forest of leaping piers, and I stagger against my mother, losing my balance amidst the noisy assault that batters my senses.

Look at the pillars around the altar, she whispers, pointing. If we were in Jerusalem at the temple we would see the same. Look at them and think you are in Jerusalem.

My reeling self steadies as I focus on one of the piers, and I notice the deep gash of the zigzag pattern winding up its length and its great width bigger than any tree I've seen, strong and unmoving, standing guard beside the altar, massive and sturdy and protecting, like my father.

Like my father was.

Then the procession enters the nave and we draw back against the wall as the monks in black pace past us, followed by priests in red and gold vestments and the Bishop-Abbot in a magnificent red cope with gold embroidery in intricate patterns and shapes wrought upon it, coming last so we know he is the most important person, but the black robes of the unimportant monks stand out more clearly against the bright noise of the walls and the jewel-glass of the windows, and the black simplicity brings relief to my senses.

And now I think you must have been among them, Thomas, as a novice, yes you are nodding, among the long line of religious, in pairs, clouded in sweet incense, pacing your way from the west end, eyes cast down, steadily slowly making your way up the long nave, and we follow from the sides, watching you separate and flow round the nave altar with its Jerusalem temple piers and through the rood screen and into the sanctuary and we cannot see you in your stalls but we can hear your sweet and sonorous chanting and we see the Bishop ascend the stone steps to his great painted throne which we *can* see, high, high above the sanctuary, high above us all.

VI

The mass begins.

Pressed against my mother's side, I listen to the priest's words of consecration chanted over the bread in the paten and the wine in the chalice, glowing gold beneath his hovering hands, words that tell how Christ's body in death becomes life to us. I hear,

Hoc est enim corpus meum . . . hic est enim calix sanguinis mei
This is my body . . . this is my blood

I kneel with the others on the cold stone and bow my head before the elements, which are no longer earthly bread and wine but Christ himself, and then I raise my head and my eyes are drawn upwards, not to the elevated host in the hands of the priest but to the great rood cross hanging above him, and as I gaze I feel as though my whole body is lifted so that I am there among Mary Jesu's mother and the Magdalene and John the disciple, clustered around the cross, and they are in desperate torment as they witness the tortured death of their beloved lord, and I gaze with them at the crucified Christ hanging, and I see yet more pain, his pain, so much pain in the drawn exhausted face and the torn, bleeding forehead and the bleeding upturned punctured palms nailed to the rood and the bent distorted nailed feet bleeding.

This pain *must* be what God wants, if even His son and all who love him are subject to it.

And a great longing rises in me to appease His gigantic anger that killed my father and so many others and put misery on my mother's face and might kill her too. God is demanding, like Marion. He will not be satisfied with the emptiness in my heart which is too dull to be called pain. I need to feel what Christ's lovers feel, what Christ himself feels, and then God might be sorry for my father's death and will protect my mother. I ask for their pains, I *beg* for them, raising my arms to Jesu hanging above me, but as I look at him and plead to him I do not think he can hear me. Like my mother, he has enough of his own pain to bear.

I feel nothing.

*

Oh Thomas, I was seven years old, and there I knelt before the suffering son of this wrathful God of my own imagining and felt that I had to appease Him all by myself, for my mother, for everyone. I was terrified and I could find no comfort. The priests of holy church taught us our God is wrath, the pestilence was proof and the pain He seemed to demand was everywhere I looked. It was a binding circle of pain, pain demanded by God, pain received from God. And I didn't think I had given or received nearly enough.

I had. I did not know it as that, but I was in deep pain, Thomas. I was seven years old and my father had died, and my too-bruised soul was hiding its unbearable loss in the darkness, beneath the empti-ness, too tender to be brought into the light and be healed. A bereaved, vulnerable soul, hiding even from herself as she tried to be strong for her mother and work out how to appease her God.

But even now the seeds were being sown that generated the visions, visions that utterly dispelled the anger I felt pressing upon me then.

*

In the night that follows I waken in the early hours, in the darkest time, and the darkness closes about me and my feeling of blame for my father's death and my terror that God might take my mother from me rise in me and I weep, muffling my sobs in my pillow, in despair at my helplessness.

Then I think, what if I were to ask not for what Christ and his lovers feel, but to come to the point of death myself? Would *that* be enough for God?

I concentrate, my tears stayed. I lie flat on my back and lay my arms across my chest like the stone knight in the chantry chapel in our church. I make myself breathe as my father did just before he died, all the way out, then waiting as long as I can before breathing in again. I do this three times, and now this breath, I tell myself, this breath is my last. The air departs from me and I let all the thoughts in my mind fall backwards into the pillow and I feel my body grow heavy and the darkness of the night grows in me and I imagine my mother sorrowful at my bedside and the curate making the sign of the cross over me and calling on my soul to repent, and I can get no further as my body demands air and the thoughts rush upwards into my mind again and I gasp and I am as alive as ever.

My body breathes and moves, shifting under the blanket, warm and alert and alive, and I think I will *never* know how to have enough pain to appease God. I toss and turn and fret. And then I sleep.

And when in the morning light I awaken and remember my failure to feel pain as I believe God wants me to feel it, I think that maybe I have to be grown up to have these feelings, that a child cannot have them. So I ask God if He would mind waiting until I am old, till I am as old as thirty, and then I will suffer all the pains He needs me to have. All of them: to come close to death myself and to feel the pain of Christ's passion as his lovers felt it and as he himself felt it. I hope that is all right. I am not sure if it is all right. I see God's eyes, which look like Marion's eyes, staring at me crossly.

But the next Sunday when we go to high mass at our own church, a Franciscan friar is visiting and preaches. He speaks gently to us, not dwelling on God's anger but on our need to learn penitence for our sins, which have brought such desolation. He speaks of Saint Cecilia who died as a martyr with three sword slashes to her neck. Three wounds. More pain! But he says we can ask for three spiritual wounds, not bodily wounds. We can ask for the wound of penitence, of contrition, to stay in our hearts always. We can ask for the wound of compassion, to feel sorry for our fellow Christians, especially for those who have died unshriven, and out of our compassion we can pray for them. And we can ask for the wound of longing for God. Our troubles should make us seek Him all the more, he says.

I bargain. If I have to wait till I am grown up to have the real pain that will appease You, God, will You accept these three wounds until then? I will try very hard to keep them. Contrition, compassion and longing for You – even though in my secret, secret heart I quail, for how can I long for one who is always so angry? But I hope God cannot see that bit of my heart.

*

And it helps, Thomas, muddled though my childish thinking was, it helps to have these three wound-vows to hang on to through the years of my childhood. I don't forget them. Indeed they grow in me mightily. But for a long time I cannot feel that they are enough for my angry God.

1353–1354

VII

I am ten years old when I see from our door a clutch of tired soldiers march past, their faces grey with exhaustion, gratefully receiving bread from my mother without breaking step, holding aloft the King's banner, faded, torn, emblazoned with St John of Beverley. We learn in the city that the wars with France have come to an end, their land and ours ravaged by the pestilence, too weary to fight and no men to send.

The sickness is passing from us, and our lives are busy once more. My mother has regained her soft round shape, though the lines on her face and the white hair beneath her wimple stay as legacies of her loss. I am growing fast but I am slender and small-boned. My long hair still tangles itself in impossible knots. We continue to live in the small-holding outside the city walls, and now Alice, who is my age, comes to stay with us to be our maid. She is taller and stronger than I, her thick black curly hair looks too wiry ever to tangle and it matches her black brows, which stand above startlingly green eyes. She is sturdy and hardworking, learning her chores quickly in the house and among the few animals and in the garden. And she joins me for lessons from my mother, who wants us both to read and write well.

*

Of all the gifts my mother gave me, Thomas, the gift of reading is the greatest.

*

Travellers pass our door, and today my mother bids me help her serve a pilgrim who has stopped for food and rest. He names himself Cyprian as he crosses our threshold and calls God's blessing on us. When he has washed and eaten good food, rye bread made fresh today by Alice, and cheese and ale, and has moved to rest in comfort by the fireside, I am allowed to come and sit on my stool and ask him questions. Alice leans against the door into the solar, quietly moving closer as he speaks so she can see and hear him better.

Where have you come from? I ask.

Rome, my daughter, he replies, his voice low, tired. The great city of Rome, across the sea and the mountains. I went to the holy Vernicle.

What is that? I ask.

The very cloth with which Saint Veronica wiped Jesu's face as he struggled to bear the great weight of the cross of his crucifixion, on the path to Calvary, the place of death.

What does it look like?

Cyprian smiles at my questioning.

I hardly know how to answer you, child, he says, but I will tell you what happened.

And his eyes look from my upturned face and gaze into the distance, seeing again as he speaks.

We were sore of foot and weary from our long journey when we arrived in the city, but other pilgrims, so many of us, were gathering to see the Vernicle because we knew it was to be displayed today, and the sweep of people carried us along. We stumbled up the steps to St Peter's hardly keeping our balance, but the size of the church before me filled me with awe and I forgot the pain in my feet and didn't mind the press of people. The noise of our prayers abated as we entered the vast space of the church, silenced by its splendour, and then swelled again as we flowed on into its deepness and clustered around a great pillar on the right-hand side. A priest at the foot of the pillar raised his hand and bade us stand still and wait. I gazed around me at the vast spaces, the roof so high I thought it must be the floor of heaven. Then I directed my thoughts to Christ and to his blessed image which I was about to see.

Cyprian's voice is trembling now and he pauses. I am caught up in his story, seeing the huge church and the great pillar and the crowd of pilgrims through his eyes, my heart beating, impatient to see more.

A cradle is let down in front of the pillar, a big cradle, with two priests in it. It sways and gently bumps against the pillar as it halts before a door, three times a man's height above the floor. The priests wait for the cradle to become quite still. Then they turn and bid us kneel, which we do, instantly becoming penitents awaiting our Lord. Someone lands painfully on my legs and he mutters an apology, shifting to one side as best he can, there is so little room.

By now Alice has crept all the way into the solar and is kneeling by me, her face as eager as mine to hear. Come *on*, Cyprian, I think. Tell us about the Vernicle. But he has paused again, and now his eyes are closed! Has he fallen asleep? Alice can bear it no longer and asks,

What happened next?

Cyprian opens his eyes and looks not at us but at the scene in St Peter's.

The priests in the cradle are murmuring prayers and moving with slow reverence as they turn back to the pillar and open the door and reach into the darkness. They move together, holding something on either side, a frame, smaller than I was expecting, no bigger than this – Cyprian holds his hands apart to show us, maybe twice the width of his lean body – and they turn, and hold it up for us.

Cyprian pauses *again* but Alice and I are silent now, watching with respect as his eyes fill with tears, and then he speaks again and his voice is still lower and more tremulous.

The Vernicle is small but we can see the blessed face of Christ clearly imprinted upon it. A sharp sound all around me echoes my own indrawn breath, sucked out of the still air by the hundreds of penitents now gazing on our Lord. I have to keep blinking away my tears and wiping my eyes to see the sharp thorns pressing on his forehead, the deep gouges in his flesh, the face distorted by pain and blood, the mouth pressed shut, the eyes gazing out at us. He is foully misused and we contemplate in deep sorrow.

This face is not as we think of the blessed and beautiful Christ in his lifetime. It is ugly.

Cyprian looks at us now, as if to emphasise his words, and I flinch inside though I hold his gaze, still looking through his eyes at what he saw.

Someone grunts, a pilgrim beside me sways in a faint, slumped but upright still, there is no room to fall and he is held by his close-pressed neighbours. Others are wailing and beating their breasts, we are a sea of devotion and love. My tears do not cease to fall as I look and look and offer the prayers I have brought all the long pilgrims' way from this land. And . . .

Cyprian stops again.

I tell you that I see the face change. I swear it changes! Maybe it is the swimming tears in my eyes. This ugly torn face looks cheerful! And then a great sadness. And now a terrible pain.

It is beautiful.

Cyprian ceases speaking and stares into the distance, blinking tears from his eyes, seeing still the holy relic, and I too can see the shape of the face and the dreadful cuts and tears in the flesh and the vile suffering, but I also see the beauty.

Alice is stock still beside me. My mother's head is bent towards Cyprian, also quite still.

We hold his seeing in our intent silence for a long time.

Presently my mother shakes herself and urges more food but Cyprian lifts his hand in refusal and rises from his seat.

I must rejoin my companions. We have further to go tonight.

And with that he walks to the door, turning only to thank us and bid us God's blessing, and I watch him swing into his pilgrim's steady pace as he leaves our house behind him and travels on, passing through lands and people, intent on God, a solitary figure hardly touched by us, touched only, transformed utterly, by his seeing.

Later, alone among the trees, I carefully and deliberately go to that place in my heart where I have put my wish to have enough pain to appease my wrathful God. This pilgrim has spoken of so much pain in his feet, in his long journey, in his weariness, and in Christ's face, Christ's actual face on the Vernicle, but the pilgrim said Christ's face was beautiful, and his own face shone as he spoke of his beloved Lord. In my mind's eye I put my wish for enough pain to appease God alongside Cyprian's face full of love. They do not fit together.

VIII

I t is the feast of Corpus Christi, when before the pestilence pageants
were performed by guilds up and down the country, and news
reaches us that they are happening again in Norwich. Many have
died in the city but it is filling again with the hungry survivors of a
forsaken countryside, seeking refuge and work. The Grocers' Guild is
bringing its play to the people and my mother says we can go.
Excitement ripples through me as we make our way across the bridge
into the city and follow the crowd to the cathedral green where a
great covered wagon stands.

I run to join the jumble of children at the front of the crowd as the
herald cries to us to be silent. Under his frowning gaze we quickly
find spaces to kneel or sit cross-legged in the grass and look up, alert-
eyed, ready to witness the great story of God's creation and the fall of
Adam.

The play begins.

God the Father, His face of gold and His clothes of finest cloth,
snowy white and billowing, enters and speaks:

I am full of joy to create the Man, Adam, and he is good, and all creation I have wrought is good, but he is alone, and that is not good. Adam must tend this garden

His arms open wide to indicate all the land around us, the whole world it seems

but he has no fit companion in this great abundance. He is lonely.

I will cause Woman to be formed.

A tall strong man enters and we gasp because he appears to be naked, but we soon see that he is clothed in fine calf-skin. Adam in the garden! We know the story so well. Adam speaks:

Truly I would welcome a companion.

God commands him to lie down. He obeys. Then he snores so we know he is asleep.

God stretches His arm out over Adam's body. He holds it there, and then raises it and as he does so we gasp again to see a woman naked in calf-skin rise up, lifted by His arm in solemn harmony of movement. She stands, and is born, drawn by God into existence. Her long hair ripples, her face radiantly smiles. Adam awakens and leaps to her side, rubbing his eyes and staring in disbelief at this beautiful companion. He clasps her to him. God beams from the side, pleased with His work. He says:

I will leave you with each other and return to my abode. Tend and keep this garden. Eat its fruits. But do not eat from the Tree of Conning of good and evil.

He points to a tree in the middle of the garden. It is a man standing with his arms aloft, hung about with leaves and fruit.

Not that tree. Never that.

God departs magnificently.

Then Adam and Eve speak to each other and delight in each other's company. They are so beautiful together I cannot take my eyes from them. They murmur, and kiss, then they turn to the garden and pretend to dig and water and prune the trees and make it even more beautiful than it already is.

When their work is done they lie together and rest. Then Adam says to Eve:

I will go for a walk on my own now. Stay and rest further, my love.

Eve smiles at him lovingly and he departs and she closes her eyes again.

We know what is going to happen next and we shiver in anticipation.

The snake appears: a slim figure in scaly dress like a fish, sparkling and shining in the sunlight, squirming on four legs across the ground towards Eve who seems to be fast asleep.

Ssssss

he says in her ear.

Ssssssister Eve, awaken, I come with a messssage.

Eve blinks and looks sleepily at the snake, whose eyes are close to hers. They have a power over her, we can see: she looks deeply into them and cannot break her gaze.

The tree, thisss tree here,

says the snake, indicating the Tree of Conning.

Will you have sssome of its fruit?

The tree man has moved forwards and now we can see the inviting bright red apples he bears, making our mouths water. Eve drags her eyes from the serpent and looks up at the tree.

We may not, she says, but her voice is dreamy, not firm.

But I have been sent by the Lord Himssself to say that you can eat of it: you mussst eat of it. It will give you powersss you can only imagine. You will know good and evil and you will be as the godsss are.

Eve is now staring into the serpent's eyes again and cannot look away. She whispers

But we may not.

You may

says the snake, his head swaying slightly. Eve's head is swaying too now, bewitched.

You musst.

He reaches up and plucks an apple, a bright shiny red apple, and holds it between Eve's eyes and his own so that she can see it while she is still under his spell.

The Lord wantsss you to

says the serpent.

Sssssister Eve, He wantsss you to. I am only Hisss messenger.

He holds the apple to her lips. It is so red and ripe and delicious looking.

Eve leans forward and takes a bite. We all gasp in horror. In her innocence she has believed a creature who claims to have come from God on His instruction, and she has obeyed the instruction.

The snake puts the bitten apple in her hand and oozes away, creeping on all fours.

Eve watches the snake leave and then wrenches her gaze from him and looks down at the apple. Slowly she rises to her feet, in an echo of her former rising into life, drawn by God. Now she is drawn by a power within her, a power given to her through the apple. She has changed. Her forehead is furrowed. She looks older, sadder, her beauty now wearing a mask of questioning and clever doubt. She holds her arms over her privacies and makes the gesture look not clumsy but noble. She shakes her hair over her face. She is beautiful still but in a completely different way, like a great noble lady who has many cares and many sadnesses, too proud to show her pain, lonely and knowing.

Adam re-enters and comes up to her. Now beside her he looks like a child or even a soft creature, with no guile.

You are awake

he says and he puts forward his head to kiss her lips but she turns away and speaks.

The serpent came to me from God, with a message to eat the fruit of the conning tree. I did, and so you must too.

He came from God.

She holds up the apple to him and without hesitation he takes it: a gift from his beautiful wife, how can he refuse? He fastens his eyes on hers and lifts the apple to his lips. We all breathe no! as he bites into it, chews and swallows.

Then his body shape changes too and he too tries to cover himself, stands taller, looks troubled and angry and in pain and proud and knowing and lost.

Eve says:

I will find us some leaves to cover our nakedness

and she goes to another tree and gathers leaves and they make themselves costumes. They do not speak as they do this. You can feel shame rising in them. They slip back amongst the trees and hide themselves.

God's voice bellows from nowhere:

Adam! Where are you? I seek you. I seek and I do not understand why I cannot see you.

He enters the stage in His gold white billowing magnificence.

Adam!

Adam and Eve emerge from the trees.

Why are you dressed thus?

We were naked and ashamed.

Adam's new-found pride is quelled and his voice is timid.

God raises both His arms – He is enormous and terrifying – and booms:

You have eaten of the conning tree! You have disobeyed Me!

Adam is querulous:

Eve told me You had required it.

Eve looks furious and scornful:

The serpent told me You had sent him.

I did not!

says thunderous God.

Come hither, serpent, thou foul creature of the devil's work.

The serpent reappears as God turns back to Adam and Eve.

I must banish you from this garden lest you eat of the tree of life and live eternally in your conning. Your banishment will be hard. You will live by the sweat of your brow and you will bring forth children in pain and labour and I will set enmity between you, Eve, and the serpent; and you, serpent, you will crawl, crawl, serpent, on your belly in the dust!

He spits this last word and the serpent falls on his belly so hard and fast that we laugh in spite of our horror at the turn of events.

Two angels enter, with large wings, brandishing equally large swords. They look cross and bossy, like Marion. They say:

Begone from this place! We will guard it against you.

Adam and Eve walk away with bowed shoulders and the serpent follows, now slithering across the ground with no legs, and the angels cross their swords and make an impregnable gate behind them.

I am crying. It is so sad.

But as I look at angry God, I can see His eyes are twinkling! He speaks softly to the couple as the gates of paradise close.

> You will enter suffering but you will be brought out again. I have plans for you.

It is the end of the play. Over the noise of clapping and cheering I try to ask the girl from the city who sits beside me what she thinks God means, but she is jumping to her feet as the crowd moves and breaks up. I stay still on the grass, thinking hard on my own, as the people about me swirl and depart.

God was angry and then twinkling, loving even. So is God only pretending to be angry?

But why did my father and so many people die in the pestilence if He is only pretending?

It wasn't really Eve's fault that they ate the apple, was it?

1361–1368

IX

I stand resistant to my mother's words.

> You are nineteen years old, a woman now, and you must marry. I
> will look for a husband for you from your father's guild.

Watching my face, which shows only too well what I think of this,
she says,

> You have a duty to bear children. Our people are stricken, we
> must have new life to bring us hope, and you are of age. And
> what else is there for you, if not marriage, than to enter a
> convent?

I see in my mind's eye a recently married woman at mass one
Sunday wearing her newly acquired, ill-fitting, heavy wimple on
her head. She wanted to linger and converse with others after the
service but her older husband did not, and he bade her come
away. Now. She had to run after him, clutching her wimple, as he
strode swiftly out of the church. She was no longer her own
mistress.

I do not want to run after a man and serve him and bear his children, and live in the city probably. But to be a nun, enclosed and silenced? Living with all those other bodies according to a rule that measures out each moment of each day?

I cannot abide either prospect. I crave my own company. I do not want to leave my home and the quiet warmth of my mother's hearth and the comfort of nature. I love my long solitary walking, listening to the trees and feeling the soft earth under my feet, beholden to none before God.

And then the pestilence returns. At first my mother and I keep away from the city, fearful of further loss, but eventually we go to mass at the cathedral, praying with others for mercy and deliverance. In the shifting crowd of worshippers I find beside me a man I think I recognise. I keep my eyes fastened on the priest but all my attention is drawn to the broad-shouldered strong presence by my side, black-haired like my father, and I feel his protection too but differently: this with longing and heat like a physical thing between us. Then I remember him: on the few occasions when I visited my father's wool house he was there as an apprentice. He does not speak to me and I will not look at him, but after the mass he falls into step with my mother and I can see, walking a short distance behind, that he is supplicating her. In spite of myself, my heart moves and the feeling is pleasurable.

Martin has a wool house of his own, says my mother when we have reached our cottage. And a merchanting business with ships that pass to Flanders with his wool.

And in the midst of the pestilence-fear for which I have little patience, foolish young woman as I am, believing my strong body to be beyond all such terrors, this trembling, the first stirrings of love for a man, bring delight and distraction. I start to think that perhaps, if Martin is kind and not overbearing, I can be his wife. I should at least find out. I consent to see him, and the stirrings of love deepen when we meet and walk together and he opens his heart to me. Beneath his strong appearance he is tender and I become comfortable in his presence. The city will be bearable if I am with him, I think.

And soon I think that everything will be bearable if only I am with him.

You are my lodestar, Martin tells me. My dear delight. My love.

He kisses me.

All present at our wedding bear amulets and charms and mutter prayers, and the restless wind whips the words from the mouth of the priest as he binds our hands in his stole and tells the world we are man and wife. The following day the wind increases to a roar, sweeping across the flat lands, splintering trees and scattering great branches like a careless giant. Within the city walls Martin and I stand in a front room of our townhouse with our arms about each other, looking out of a window, watching loosened thatch fly and unstable chimneys threaten to fall. Then a more distant, distinct and thunderous *crack!* sounds and we clutch each other more tightly as we see the tall wooden spire of the great cathedral sway violently, topple and fall with a great crash, disappearing out of our sight.

The shock of the spire's destruction shakes an already weakened people to the core. How much wrath must God harbour! How much more can we bear? What worse sins have been committed and by whom? Who is responsible for this? But Martin and I spend the first days of wedlock clearing debris and laughing, defiant, invincible, unconcerned.

X

Our city home is comfortable and spacious, with a large hallway and solar, a separate room for dining, a room for official business, a cook house and privy in their own buildings in the yard, and bedchambers upstairs. But the yard is small and paved and fetid and surrounded by a high stone wall. It is our only outside space in the cramped city.

I learn to direct the household, managing the accounts and writing such letters and testimonies as are needful. I become diligent in the work of a merchant's wife. But although I love Martin he is often not present, and I do not love this life, my slender, active body all day cramped inside the weighty clothes and headdress of a married woman, inside a house, inside a city, the walls bearing upon me, standing fast between me and nature's wildness, the servants of the household requiring direction, the endless daily tasks. I am tyrannised by lists, composing them, discharging them, directing others with them; I see them in my sleep.

I am busy in my new life but, upon discovering there are books I can borrow, copies of stories of the saints and more, reading gives me some interior space where I can again tend the wound-vows I asked for as a child. I had not realised how present they had been to me on my walks in the forests and fields of my childhood home, running through my head with my thoughts and repeating with the beats of my heart: contrition, compassion, longing for God, wounds that kept me open to the world around me and to God. Now they present themselves afresh, taught by the saints I read about. I have missed them.

There is little time for my reading and solitary prayer, and it is not a pastime that Martin approves or shares; he does not wish to hear the thoughts my practice stirs in me.

Today I am deep in my book, reading about Saint Margaret of Antioch who consecrated herself to Christ and refused to marry. She was wounded, tortured and killed for her faithfulness, performing many miracles before she died. I am deep in her world, wondering at her rejection of the householder's life, questioning my own acceptance of it, wondering about my childhood vows, especially the last. Can I truly long for God as a distracted, busy merchant's wife? Despite her torture, I envy Margaret's unswerving devotion.

A touch on my shoulder startles me and I look up, unseeing, still deep in my thoughts. Then my vision clears to see Martin looking down at me. He is smiling but the smile is terse and I can see suppressed irritation in his eyes.

Mistress, your household needs you, he says.

He speaks mildly, but a second tap on my shoulder is strong. I hastily rise and attend to him. He says nothing further on the matter but I understand it should not happen again, and fear I must forfeit my reading. But John, our journeyman and steward, has noticed my habit of retreating to a corner of the solar with my back to the room whenever I can, and sees Martin's impatience. One morning when we meet to go over the tasks for the day he says quietly

Mistress, there will be an hour before our midday meal for you to read.

He speaks without looking up at me, but nods his head, a smile touching the corners of his mouth, and from then on he tries to make space for me to be left alone whenever he can. It is not my wish to join forces with John to deceive Martin, but we both know that the time for my reading must be found when he is not by.

Once, when taking some written accounts from me, John's fingers touch mine. A momentary brushing past, I do not know if it is deliberate. I am busy and swiftly move on to other tasks, but my fingers remember his touch.

XI

I am as I should be with Martin in the bedchamber, but the soft kisses and gentle delight in our bodies all too swiftly settle into tired lovemaking because it is our duty. In due course I become a mother. The birth of Lora, my child, my beautiful daughter, is bloody.

Your child does not wish to leave the safety of your womb, the midwife tells me

as I struggle for hours to release her from me, the pain in my body growing and my weariness growing as with each contraction I push and strain and heave. She finally shoulders herself into the world, tearing herself free from my body, blood and water and pain her bearers, in that intense and mercifully swift moment of birth. My body is torn and bleeding and exhausted, but when the new-swaddled child is placed in my arms my pains recede and my spirit comes alive as I gaze at my daughter. I look into her wide eyes and feel love take root deep within me, growing and expanding to embrace her and all that she will become, stretching far into the future. I am already protective of her young bones and her venturing out of doors on her own, indignant at her choice of husband, delighting in my grandchildren.

We will fill our house with children,

declares Martin in his rich expansive voice and I smile, but my heart sinks.

To my relief and Martin's regret, I do not again fall pregnant. But Lora grows bright-faced, raven-haired, strong-boned and interested in everything, pestering me with questions and wanting to learn and join in whatever I am engaged with. I love her with all my heart, but I am not a good mother. Now to the endless business of the household is added the pestering of a child. There is no time for the solace of books. Each night I fall on my knees in penitence at my shortening temper and sharpening tongue; each morning I arise and I am worse. I feel a prisoner. I see how my daughter is sensitive as I was, and I see her flinch at my harsh words, and when I come to myself before God in my prayers I weep for the feelings she will feel and the hurt she will sustain. I want to protect her as much from myself as from the world.

Her father is often away with his merchanting, bringing stories from Flanders where we sell our wool, but when he is with us I can see he too feels her tender soul and longs to keep his strong arms around her to stay any harm. He kindles my penitence as I watch him laugh with her, tumbling on the rushes playing bear, looking up at me with a huge smile, wanting to include me in his happiness and protecting care. He should protect her from me, I think.

And only now does it occur to me to ask my mother why she, also a merchant's wife, did not carry the burdens I carry. How was it that I grew up in peace in a smallholder's cottage, the woods and fields my playground, when we, and every merchant's family I know, are imprisoned in the city, with Lora's growth cramped by its walls and my impatience?

I could not abide it, my mother confesses when I visit her and ask. I was not from merchanting stock and I could not get used to the life. I could not keep the books nor govern the servants; after you arrived I did not fall pregnant again: I was failing in every part of the life I should lead as a merchant's wife. I lost my health and my looks and I . . . I began to hate your father who had brought me to this. I blamed him for my suffering, all of it.

I swore to your father that if we did not leave the city together I would leave alone.

I marvel at my mother's strength and courage. It would have been her ruin if she had abandoned her family as she threatened. But she must have meant it or my father would not have managed his business without having his household nearby, and found a cottage outside the walls so she could grow our food, tend our few animals, stretch her limbs and her heart, and I could wander freely under a big sky.

It was not just my stubbornness, adds my mother, smiling a little. I made my request when you were two years old, in the year the crops failed. Famine threatened us all and your father could see the sense in ensuring we had our own food to grow and eat. He negotiated the use of this smallholding with the landowner and moved his family here.

Then she speaks more quietly.

But our move has meant that you, too, are not prepared for the merchant's life. And you are changing as I changed.

We see reflected in each other's eyes the realisation that yes, I am treading the path my mother trod. I can feel the love I have for Martin already cooling in my heart. Will it grow warm again, not as love but as resentment and hatred?

Martin is a good man but I do not think he will bring his family outside the city.

I leave my mother in her quiet cottage under the trees and walk slowly back to my prison, its walls closing about me as my despairing inward eyes see them only pressing further upon my trapped soul as the years roll past.

1369–1370

1369–1570

XII

D ear Thomas, your eyes are full of pity for that desolate young mother. Perhaps you know what happens next. The pestilence strikes again. And this time it presses upon us and does not pass on; we are caught in the trap of our house in the centre of the city. Martin refuses to stay within, returning every day to his warehouse, and I grow more and more angry with him as the dangers increase and he does not seem to care. Lora is fractious, as like me she does not wish to be held and yet I keep her and myself inside, fulfilling my duties to my endless lists, trying to keep her occupied. Unable to prevent Martin from bringing the threat of infection into our home, I insist on fumigating the house daily with lit thyme, and Martin too, making him stand in the hallway when he returns from his pestilent warehouse, eyes smarting as I wave the smoking leafy twigs over every part of him.

I try my hardest to be patient. But one day when Martin has been gone on business for a week, when Lora is crosser than ever and John has argued with me, when my orders to fumigate the house have not been followed, when the clouds are low and threatening thunder, when the stink of the city encroaches, I cannot abide to be trapped within this hell any longer, and I walk out.

Out of the house, out of the city, across the river, and I keep walking till I am among the trees and I can pull off my wimple and shake my hair free and, at last, breathe clean, fresh air.

I stay alone with the trees for hours. I think that if I can come to myself I can pray and if I can pray I can return to my life in the city and I can bear it. I grant myself this time, even as the thunder rumbles and rain starts to fall and the heaviness in the air lifts and the heaviness in my heart is lifted.

When I finally return, just before I enter the house I look up at the eaves. Rain pours from the drenched thatch and splashes on my upturned face once more enclosed by my now wringing-wet wimple. I remember that moment so well, Thomas. It is the last moment of ease I have for a long time.

XIII

The stench comes first. Sour vomit and rotting flesh stinking the dim hallway. Where is everyone? I cross the silent hall, my heart thumping, following the smell that strengthens with every step towards the solar. And as I reach the threshold I hear a quiet whimpering, and then I see the body, Martin's body, prostrate on the floor, pus seeping through his damp clothes, leaking with his vomited blood into the rushes, his downturned face in a mucky puddle of spew and blood – and there is Lora! Crouching in the far shadows, arms cradling his head, eyes wide and fixed on her father, stock still, in an abominable distortion of Mary with her dead son Jesu in her arms, a daughter not a mother holding her father not her son, so small, so helpless, so wrong! On the instant I run to her and clasp her to me, pulling her from the weight of the foul-smelling, heavy body, pushing Martin's head to one side without thinking of what I am doing, drawing my cold, trembling, whimpering, horror-struck daughter away from this place.

I carry her upstairs to her bedchamber. I think Martin must be dead but I do not stop to find out, nor do I call through the silent house to summon John or the absent servants to help him. My whole being is wrapped around my cold child and there is room for nothing and no one else.

Lora will not speak until I have made her drink some milk heated and infused with sage, sitting in the chair beside her bed and holding her in my lap and stroking her hands and her hair and finally the words come.

I did not know where you were, she says. I was waiting in the hall, listening for you. You did not come. You did not come. And then the door crashed open and father was standing there and I was so happy to see him and so excited because I was not expecting him home, but his face was all wrong and he smelled so horrible and then he moved and I had to run backwards into the solar as he stumbled towards me and I wanted to help him but I wanted to be sick and then he tripped and I jumped away or he would have fallen on me but then *I* fell backwards on my bottom and he landed with his head on my lap and I couldn't move. Oh! I did not know what to do! I wanted to help him, mother, I wanted to help him and you were not there and I felt so sick and I was so frightened!

She weeps, then, great wracking sobs and I hold her tightly, forbidding my own thoughts, murmuring soft words. I tell her that her father is in heaven with the angels – he must be dead by now, I think, my heart moving with guilt towards him for a moment – and that God has made him whole and Christ has enfolded him in his love, and after a while her tears dry and her eyes shine brightly. Too brightly. Then she slackens in my arms and I can feel sleep overcoming her. I lay her down carefully in her bed and cover her quiet body.

And I am left with my guilt. I abandoned my household and let my daughter face what I had faced when I was just her age, only worse – far, far worse. How could I not have thought this might happen? I should have protected Lora from this harrowing repeated fate.

The smell awakens my senses and drags me from my self-reproach. I must attend to Martin. I go downstairs and make myself enter the solar to look at his body. He is still lying with his head as I had pushed it to free Lora, and I am certain he is dead. I think of his unshriven soul. He had no priest to absolve him, but I have told Lora he is in heaven and I say this out aloud for her and for him,

> Sweet Mary, mother of our Lord Jesu Christ, pray for my husband's soul before almighty God, that his sins may be forgiven and he may enter heaven with the saved.

I have no idea if this is right or if it will work but the smell is so bad now I have to move away and find help. Where *is* John? Have the servants all fled? I search deserted rooms until I hear quiet repetitive muttering from the back yard, and discover the maid Rose cowering, holding a lavender bag to her nose and swaying with her prayers. I gentle her as best I can to come within and help me draw a blanket over the body. We do so, our mouths covered. She is brave; I have to be. Then my heart leaps with relief as I hear John's voice calling from the front of the house. He comes swiftly through to us.

> Leave, Rose, he says, pushing her out of the door and turning to me. Mistress, go to Lora, is she abed? Go to her. I will deal with Martin's body. Go!

I go, and remain upstairs stroking Lora's hair as she sleeps, listening to the men taking Martin away and instructing John to keep the family within for a week. We must stay apart till the pestilential air has gone from us, they say.

The next day we scrub and fumigate the house but only John is there to work with me. Rose has fled with the other servants. Lora wants to help but she is listless and does not quarrel when I bid her rest. In the evening she sits by the fire, her eyes fixed on the flames. She will not look up at me and when it is time to eat she has no appetite. She walks stiffly and although she does not make a sound I can see from her face and the tightening around her eyes and mouth and her sharp, indrawn breath that she is in pain. She looks much older than her six short years.

In the night I go to her bedchamber. She sleeps, though her breathing sobs as if she were crying, and her cheeks are bright. Too bright. Gently, without disturbing her, I feel her armpits. There are swellings. And her groin, and there are swellings.

I take myself to the solar. I sit down carefully and I clasp my hands together. I pray. I do not think I have the strength for this. It will be a very few days, then she too will be gone.

How will I bear it?

Because you must.

Late though it is, John is awake, standing in the doorway. I have spoken aloud without knowing it, and he answers, steady as he has always been.

You must, and you will. You have strength enough and more. I will help you.

I look at him with gratitude as resolve rises in me. I can, I *will* walk towards the pain that is coming.

Dawn is stealing across the floor and over Lora's restless body when I return to her side. She wakens and turns to me and looks straight into my eyes; she knows the pestilence has come to her. I place my hand on her hot forehead, then carefully lift a stray curl of hair and smooth it back on her head. I am gentle and smiling and quiet, but within me my heart is torn to shreds as I watch my beloved daughter suffering and I am impotent to take the sickness from her. I would bear it myself.

If only I could take it from her and bear it myself.

At my direction John sends for oil of lily and I gently rub it into the swellings, bringing some relief from the foul smell. And though I hate to do it, I make her swallow mustard that will make her vomit. I hold her hair away from her head as she heaves and retches and the bile leaps from her small body, but the fever grows in her and she begins to mutter mad words, walking through worlds I do not recognise. She does not know me. She struggles against the physic but is too weak to put off my determined ministering.

I ask John to try and find a priest for Lora, but the messenger he sends cannot find one who will come to our stricken, quarantined house.

The day passes. By the evening the boils on her body have begun to burst, great brown and green foul-smelling gobs of pus emerging.

John brings more water and cloths and I clean and comfort her but my daughter's mind has gone from me and she raves to others whom only she sees. It is midnight before her restless cries and movements are stayed. Now her body is bathed in sweat and furnace hot to touch. I wrap her in a blanket soaked in cold water but she is as feverish afterwards as before.

There is no priest. I kneel by my dying daughter and carefully trace a cross on her hot forehead, on her muttering lips and on her heaving breast.

I say

and I believe

Almighty God absolves you of your sins.

Early morning lights the second day, and she is quiet, and she quietly dies.

XIV

I do not know how long I sit as one in a trance, feeling nothing, my hand stayed on my dead daughter's chest. Then John appears and suddenly I cannot bear a single thing, not one thing more, and I run from the room, down the stairs and out into the yard, and fall on my knees. I can hear a wailing moan and I know it is mine though I do not feel myself making it.

How much pain do You need, God?

How much pain? Is this enough for You now? Is this *enough*?

I stare with eyes like sand at a tiny plant growing between two wall stones, a growing thing that lives while my daughter is dead upstairs, my beloved daughter who tore my body and now tears my heart in pieces, who has passed through her own foul tunnel of illness and pain, is dead, dead.

The straggling plant lives, and is silent.

She touched his body, breathed his breath!

Martin! Why did you bring death to us? *Why* did you insist on going out into the pestilential world? Did it matter to you more than your family? You, you whom I loved and served, you who did not mean to but became my gaoler, you went out. I stayed, I *stayed*, Martin . . .

The silent, living plant stares back at me, and now it seems to me it is God's emissary and it accuses not Martin, but me.

Is it because I could not stay? Wandering among the trees in the rain, glorying in my stolen freedom, wimple-free, list-free, household-free . . .

I hang my head before the pitiless plant.

Daughter-free.

Guilt lays itself like a heavy blanket over my anger. If I had not abandoned my household and my duties, would Martin and Lora have been saved?

I will never know. All I can know is that that is what I did; and while I was wandering among the trees in the rain my husband was dying and my daughter had to witness his death and cradle his body and she was alone.

The plant lives, and reproaches me.

Now the anger boils up again and the guilt boils up with it and they battle with each other and roar till I think I will explode and I am shouting at the silent growing plant with no answers and now I am pulling at it and then pummelling it against the stone wall till it is utterly destroyed and my fists are bleeding and I kneel there, looking at my fists, sobbing, helpless, a child longing for her father to come and make everything all right. And now the long pent-up grief for *his* death breaks in me and joins the grief for my daughter and the grief for my husband, pouring through me like a river in spate, gathering my anger and my guilt into its waters as it swells and thunders and I kneel, drowning in loss, my bloody fists smearing my tunic as I hold myself tightly, because I think I will fall apart, there is so much loss.

They are coming, God, I whimper, they are coming

and then my inner voice grows strong as the anger and the guilt and the pain gather together to batter the doors of heaven on their behalf and roar at the heavenly host: they are coming, my daughter, my father, my husband; they are Yours now. Fold them in Your company and grant them joy. Grant them the fullest joy. The fullest joy. Joy. And now the tears fall full and fast and I soften and there is only pain and it enters my soul and floods into every corner of my being and I cannot understand why I am still alive.

XV

In the time that follows I move as one who is walking through thick slime. The air is heavy, my body is heavy, every task is a burden to me and every person I meet is a stranger. I have nothing to live for and I do not wish to live. Some servants return, the household revives a little, the merchanting begins again under John's direction, but I eat only because the maid brings me food and I direct the household only because John stands in front of me and waits patiently for my orders. Kind-hearted and understanding and attentive, he does what he can to relieve me, remaining strong so I can be weak. I do not know what to do or how to be.

After a time I lift myself from my torpor and I wander outside through silent streets still empty of citizens, grateful for the quiet while hating its cause. My steps take me to the cathedral where I am alone and anonymous, hidden in the shadows, and there I return again and again, standing for long hours dry-eyed, murmuring dry prayers, gazing upon a wall painting of St Thomas wrapped in his green cloak, kneeling with his hand in Christ's wounded side, his face upturned and penitent. I gaze and my fingers tell my prayer beads, repeating *Ave Maria*, Hail Mary, *Pater Noster*, Our Father, and my prayer is barren, barren, but it directs my angry, guilty, painful thoughts to other words, words of repentance, words that pray for mercy, for forgiveness though I do not deserve it. I do not know the God whom I supplicate. I do not know who God is.

Thomas! This latest pitiless wave of pestilence took our young men and our children from us, our children, and robbed us of hope. But the priests do not spare us, saying again that it is punishment for our guilt and what have we done and who is to blame?

I am to blame. I am. Bereaved and lost as I am, I feel my guilt in my heart and I do not spare myself. But nor do I know how to atone. I cannot bear any more pain and I do not know what else to offer if not that, for the God who has shown Himself to me seemed only to demand pain, and He has been given what He asked for, and now He is silent.

XVI

A year has passed and custom expects that I put away my widow's garments. Indeed it is my duty. I should not stand in the shadows with only prayer beads to occupy my hands. It is reasonable and right to seek another husband, to have more children if I am able, and to care for the wealth Martin has left me. And John, who has been so faithful and attentive since the day I arrived in Martin's house, who did not desert me when Martin died and the servants fled, to whom I can never be grateful enough, begins to move forward from the shadows of his long regard. Not at first with words but by small gestures that I cannot help but read. Though I need no assistance, he holds out his hands to help me from my chair. He looks at me for longer than is necessary when we eat together. He stays seated at the table after we have finished discussing the business of the day, silent, as though waiting for something.

John is a good man. There are few enough husbands to come by now the pestilence has taken so many of our young men from us, and most women would not hesitate to encourage John's hints that we might be more to each other than steward and mistress. But much as I care for him and am grateful to him, I feel only dull and listless when I consider the prospect of renewing my householder's life. And as the thought that I might bear another child moves through my mind, the costly pain of love and loss twists in me again. No. I do not want more children. And my heart does not lift when I think of John, dear though he is to me, necessary though he is to my welfare, living in this great house in the city as I am.

This day when our business is complete and John has again stayed sitting at the table in silence, he looks up, his eyes big with hope.

Mistress, I would speak what is in my heart, he begins.

My own heart moves a little in my breast. Only a little, and not with pleasure. I do not want John to go on, but he does.

I am but a poor substitute for Martin in his – your – business and an even poorer substitute for his companionship . . .

I lift my eyes to his, imploring him to stop, but he does not see what is in them, or if he does he is too intent on his own purpose and continues

But I dare to hope that I might . . . one day . . .

his voice falters as I give him no encouraging smile, no gesture to welcome his words

Be more to you than . . .

He stops again and this time does not try to continue. I remain silent, completely still, my eyes upon his, but in truth I am not looking at him; I am reading what is deep within myself.

Painted over every inch of the walls of my heart is the terrible guilt I feel for abandoning my family and I do not believe I have a right to joy.

Behind the guilt, deeper than that, I know that the householder's life would not bring me joy. It never did.

Undeserving as I am, should I consent to marry John *because* it will be a joyless life of duty?

I look at John and I think: you are a good man, and I love you for your care of Martin's business and the household and for your care for my daughter's welfare and my own. Yes, I truly love you for this service. And I am fearful of giving up the security our marriage would bring. But I do not desire you, and I do not desire your world and if I consent to it in order to deny myself joy, I would deny you joy also and you do not deserve that.

And I move even more deeply within myself and I learn that I will never again be a householder for the sake of a man and I stay with that knowledge because it is true, though it scares me.

The silence is growing between us.

Into the silence John says

You know what I am asking

and rises clumsily from his seat. I watch his strong back as he departs. I know what I do not want, but nothing of what I do.

XVII

I leave the city to visit my mother, seeking her comfort though I think she will not understand my reluctance to accept John's hand and I fear she may try to persuade me otherwise. But I am surprised by her. After two days of blissful solitary walking among familiar trees and along the steadfastly flowing river, and sitting quietly with her by the fireside in the evenings, spinning and speaking only as we feel and not because we should, she says,

Child, you must make up your mind, and put John's heart at rest.

Defensive tears start. I say,

You do not understand. I hardly understand myself! I do not want John's hand. I do not want to live again as I did with Martin. You saw what it was doing to me! You were blessed with a husband who brought you here. Mine would not. And I abandoned him, I abandoned my daughter. You did not abandon your family and I did, I did! I cannot—

I cease to speak – my tears are falling fast now – and I cover my face with my hands, sobbing like the child I feel I am once more.

My mother rises and kneels by my spinning stool and draws me to her.

Shh, shh there, my dear; there there, my dear. Dry your tears.

She tucks my loose hair into my wimple.

There, my dear. I am not going to tell you to accept John's hand.

I draw back and look at her in astonishment.

No?

No. But if you have decided that you do not want him, you must tell him. Set him free to seek the hand of another.

Tears of relief. But then, childlike still, I wail

What will I do with myself? I cannot live in that house and run Martin's business on my own.

That is true, says my mother, calmly resuming her stool and her spinning. So why don't you give John the merchant business and warehouse, and ask for a pension in exchange? Come and live here for the time being. Alice will be glad of your presence and so will I. What is in store for you will be shown to you when you are ready. We will see what the future holds in God's good time.

I sit back on my stool and regard my mother with new eyes. She speaks decisively, as a woman unbound by convention, free before God to make up her own mind and her own life.

I would love to do that, I say. But I did not expect you to offer.

Remember I did not remarry either, after your father died, she replies. It was risky, deciding to remain in the smallholding with no man for protection, with only you and Alice for company. But the landowner told me I was welcome to stay for as long as I wished. I love this life. I did not think there would be another who would marry me on terms so hard won from your father, and I was not prepared to forswear them, so I took the risk. And over these many, many years, I have gained greater confidence in my own judgement. I do not see why you should not do the same.

She nods at me.

Spin, daughter. We need the wool. And I want to tell you about a community of lay women who live on Elm Hill, by St Peter Hungate in the city. For some time now I have visited them. They have neither married nor taken the veil, but live together soberly, praying together, caring for the poor in the city, and they earn their keep as parchmenters. It is permitted for women to have such a trade. And they are studious, they copy books and read together.

My time with these good women has set my heart at rest about the future. I think you will like to meet them. You may find comfort there, as I have done.

*

The next day I return to the city house which already no longer feels mine. As I walk, I think: I will speak to John and then I will leave and not return. If I borrow a horse from the warehouse I can load it with my things and bring them home with me today. Alice can take the horse back.

Though I should have been, I am not prepared for John's reaction. I had half wondered if he sought my hand only because he desired Martin's business. Offered it without my hand he is not grateful but harsh, angry.

> Do you know what you are giving up? Wealth, comfort, protection, family around you? You will be lonely. Bored, with no one to care for. What will you do with yourself all day? You could have children to love and to keep you as you grow old. For you *will* grow old, mistress, and infirm, and unable to care for yourself.

I remain silent. I cannot argue with him, I have no answers. The life I seek has none of John's proffered comforts and I have not seen yet what it will have, so what can I say, except, after a short while, with a small and helpless gesture

> I-I need to pack my things. May I borrow a horse? We will return it.

And John nods impatiently and returns to his accounts.

When the horse is loaded I go back to say goodbye for the last time. As I turn to go John rises suddenly from his table, his, now, not mine, and moves close to me, too close, and now his hand is on my shoulder, holding it fast. He forces my body round to face him and looks at me hard, his eyes blazing, and he says,

Think very hard before you spurn me, for I shall not ask you again.

The grip on my shoulder is strong and protective and full of longing. And for a moment I think I am mistaken to abandon the security of John's love, which I see is good and true to its core, for the sake of a future full of uncertainty. But only for a moment. I never again want to be burdened with the house and the servants and the business and the money. And I leave without looking back.

1370–1373

XVIII

Regret never replaced the relief in my heart after I left, Thomas. My mother's tranquillity taught me, and I felt in myself I was being true to my own calling, even if it showed itself only in what it was not. In her soft company, with few distractions, I discovered how much confusion and pain I still had, subject to sudden shocking waves of anger and guilt which rolled through me, catching me off guard and leaving me incapable of thought or movement, pain which had me curling up like a babe and silently howling till the storm passed.

*

After some weeks, my mother brings me to a large house on Elm Hill, just above the cathedral, to meet the lay sisters who have so transformed her. It is a steep climb on a warm morning, and we are red-faced when we reach the front door. We wait to catch our breath before knocking and I hear sounds inside, a scraping noise, snatches of song and, just as my mother raises her hand to knock, a burst of laughter. At the rap of knuckles the laughter stops and so does the scraping noise, and a few moments later the door opens. A tall, big-boned woman with thick hair spilling from a workman's cap and a large apron tied over a simple brown dress stands before us, barefoot, still chuckling.

Margaret!

My mother is smiling broadly even as she says,

We have mistimed our visit: you are all working still.

Nay, Johanna, you are always welcome. We are just finishing for the morning. If only my sisters were more efficient at their task we would be done by now.

Margaret ushers us within, wagging her finger in mock censoriousness at her fellow workers. We find ourselves in a workshop that takes up the entire ground floor of the house, lit by big open doors at the far end. One deep shelf bears rolls and square-cut sheets and sewn books of parchment, another, tools; further back, where the light is stronger, three wooden frames holding stretched-out animal hides lean against the limewashed walls. Two women stand in front of a frame each, aproned and barefoot like Margaret, holding scraping knives and sandblocks, stalled in their work as they laugh at their sister's admonitory finger, and smile at us.

Berta, Felicia! Johanna has come to visit, and she has brought . . .

Margaret turns to my mother.

Julian. This is Julian, my daughter.

I step forward, feeling shy.

Julian. Welcome! Take her upstairs, Johanna. Matilda is already there, preparing our meal. We will finish here and then we can all go to mass before we eat.

Before I follow my mother up the stairs in the far corner of the workshop I glance through the open doors, seeing a frame with a wet skin stretched and drying in the sun, and past it the hill that rises steeply behind the sisters' house to a church which must be St Peter Hungate. At the top of the stairs we find ourselves in a large open area with a table and six chairs for eating to the left of a central fireplace and two comfortable settles covered in bright cushions to the right. The space is flooded with noonday light. The smell of food is delicious.

Just . . . let me . . . stir this . . . There. Our meal will be ready to eat after mass.

Matilda straightens up from the fireplace where she is tending a round pot hanging over a banked-up fire, and carefully smooths the creases in her dress before she turns to us.

Johanna, you are most welcome. And this is . . .?

My daughter Julian.

Moments later the workers call that they are ready and we rejoin them to climb together to St Peter's. The women are a quiet presence at the mass in their simple brown habits and sandalled feet. As we move to leave the church at the end, the priest stands in our way. By the sisters' reaction I understand that this happens often, as I see them stop without surprise and wait patiently for him to speak.

You are all well, I trust?

he asks, not unkindly, but looking carefully into each of their faces.

Yes, Father, says Felicia.

And these are . . .? indicating my mother and myself.

Mother and daughter, Johanna and Julian. Both sober widows, says Felicia quickly, as though anticipating his next question.

Our food is awaiting us, says Matilda, and she smiles and moves determinedly forward. We must feed our guests.

Of course, says the priest, stepping aside with reluctance. I just wanted to tell you, Berta, of another widow, named Lucy, who has moved to live close by your riverside workshop and is in great need. Will you attend her?

Of course, says Berta, and moves off with the rest of us.

We return to the house and eat Matilda's delicious pottage made with oats and barley, carrots, onions and a little meat, seasoned with herbs. The sisters converse easily with each other and my mother joins in, speaking with more confidence and wit than I have seen in her before. I am quiet, quietly observing, quietly absorbing the intelligent warmth of the company I am in.

After we have finished our meal, Berta, Margaret, Matilda and my mother take baskets of food and leave to visit Lucy and the many others in the city who are in need of their help. Felicia and I clear and clean the table and the bowls and spoons, and then she invites me to sit on one of the settles, taking her place on the other.

Johanna has spoken a little of you, says Felicia, so we know something of your life. I am sorry for your troubles.

She pauses, but I cannot speak, for in this sympathetic, easy warmth I find my throat is choked and tears tremble in my eyes, threatening to fall fast. Felicia seems to understand, and instead of questioning me, she says,

Would you like me to tell you how we came to live this life together?

All I can do is nod. Her voice is low and gentle, its tone as much as her words a balm to my unsteady heart.

We found each other, the four of us, in the year of the storm that destroyed the spire of the cathedral. We were in our different ways looking for a life that had companionship and holiness but not the vows and strictures of the clothed religious. So we decided we would try to create the life we wanted ourselves.

Our allegiance is to God and to each other and we are free as holy church would not have us. But we have persisted in our life and now we are respected.

She pauses.

Mostly.

Our day begins early, with prayer and breaking our fast together, then each morning we work at our parchmenting, as you saw, sometimes here where the stretching and dry scraping is done, sometimes down by the river where we have a wet workshop for cleaning and preparing the hides before bringing them up here for treatment. We sell rolls of parchment, and we also cut them or fold and sew them into books ready for the scribe's pen. When there is time we copy texts ourselves.

Felicia smiles suddenly.

I love to write. I was blessed to be taught by scholars and while I am clumsy in the workshop, I am deft with a pen. Sometimes Margaret, who is in charge of the parchmenting, loses patience with my feeble scraping and sends me in disgrace to a corner bench to copy a text and that pleases me beyond anything. Margaret is skilled at her work but she is clumsy enough with a pen, as I remind her if she becomes too overbearing. And she is not good at finishing the parchments to the standards required by our customers. Matilda is best at that.

After mass and our midday meal, we go to the city to care for the poor and that is where Berta is most herself and most effective. She is tender with the poor widows struggling in our city and even if we have not much to give them, they are always comforted by her.

We return to pray together before our evening meal, and then comes my favourite time, when we gather here in our solar and read to each other. We speak of what we read and of any good preaching or teaching we have heard; we always go to listen when a friar visits the city, willing to share his knowledge. We are hungry to learn. Well, I am!

Holy church does not know what to make of us, women who are neither enclosed as nuns nor married. We are too independent, we do not fit. But we are mostly left alone, especially as we are seen daily by the priest at St Peter's. He keeps an eye on us, as you saw.

Felicia laughs, but then she frowns a little.

Is the priest very intrusive? I ask.

But my words are lost in a deep yawn, and to my dismay my eyes are closing and I cannot stop them.

Felicia looks at me and smiles. She does not seem surprised at my reaction and nor does she seem to think me rude, as she rises and carefully removes my shoes and helps me lie flat on the soft settle, placing a cushion under my head.

Your soul is weary, Julian, she says, and softly moves away and goes downstairs.

I watch her quietly depart as my body succumbs to the comfort of the settle and the warmth of the sun, drowsily admiring these women who seem so contented with their self-determined life.

I sleep more deeply than I have done for a long time, and I do not waken until the sisters have all returned.

Johanna has gone home, they tell me, but she knows you are with us and if you wish you need not leave until the city curfew at dusk. They are so untroubled by me that I remain entirely at rest, sitting up to join with their prayers, staying to eat a simple evening meal of bread and cheese and milk, and because the evening remains light, staying to hear their reading and their conversation.

XIX

I am smitten by my new friends. Felicia, Berta, Margaret and Matilda include me in their work and their prayers and study without fussing over me, naturally enfolding me and warming me with their company as they have my mother. Soon I am with them nearly every day from the time the city gates open until they close again at night.

Berta is round and comfortable and crumpled, soft as rabbit fur, laughing as the dirty child in her arms pulls at the hair coming loose from her wimple, smiling over his head at his mother who, desolate without a husband or her other children, cannot help but smile back. Margaret, in charge of the parchmenting, is strong-boned and skilled, her large competent hands scraping and sanding the animal hides easily and steadily, big limbs clumsy and awkward everywhere except at her work. She directs us in the same strenuous task but our efforts are never as satisfactory and Matilda, assistant parchmenter, fusses at our uneven finishes. Matilda is always neat and tidy, careful with her clothes; the simple brown dress all the sisters wear looks as though it was made for her. But Felicia, scholar, scribe and deep thinker, becomes my special companion. Her mind is sharp as a pin, she is ascetic, straight-backed, always a little cleft of concentration frowning between her dark brows until a sister grasps an argument in a book we are reading, and then she suddenly smiles and her face is radiant. I can listen for hours to her thoughts about the texts we read and the sermons we hear.

The sisters are steady in their chosen life, but the city is not. Our afternoons are filled with the needs of others as we traverse the streets of Norwich, attending to the poverty-stricken, beached survivors of the pestilence-wave that has rolled through our world, meeting child-lost widows with blank eyes and leaden hearts, struggling to find ways to earn a livelihood. In the houses and marketplaces we find all the loss and longing and deep grief and guilt that echo so strongly in my own heart. A blanket of mourning is laid across the city, muffling the lives of all, even as we strive to return to what we were. The great gaping holes do not easily close over. Labourers are few and merchants like John search for men to work for them. New life brings desperately needed solace and hope. Children are born, even to women who believed themselves no longer fertile. But the city mourns, and at the daily mass in St Peter's and at Sunday high mass in my mother's church I sometimes feel the pain swell so strongly it is as though the hearts of the gathered people are moaning out loud, sharp splinters of pain passing like a physical thing through us.

We must endure till the sharp-edged pain is dulled. But I carry in my heart the wound of my own guilt, Thomas, and that never heals, even as my great grief grows bearable. My childhood vow of contrition is powerfully honoured now in my penitence. I feel no worth in me, but my sorrow softens me towards others and grows sympathy in me. And so my second vow of compassion is honoured. I deserve nothing and the people deserve their pain to be soothed and so, taught by Berta, I give my softness to them. And truth to tell, my heart is eased as it opens itself to strangers.

And every day, as I feel my contrition bite and my compassion expand, I hear my third vow to long for God. But my God remains aloof, angry with me. I am like a child seeking comfort from her parents for she has nowhere else to turn, and I raise my arms to Him as a child would, like the bereaved child that I was, but I do not feel His love reaching down to me in response. I do not feel any response, only distant anger like the distant rumbling of thunder as a storm approaches. My soul is unable to bear admonition, it is soft and tender like a bruised fruit, so if He is angry it is better He stays far from me, I think, though it leaves me desolate. At this time I cannot bear to be handled, as a battered body cannot bear the touch of others, even when gently intended, and my God is not gentle. But I have nowhere else to go, and though I feel nothing of God's love, I feel the sisters' love and so I feel something of safety. I believe that the daily presentation of my sorry soul to God at mass by fastening my eyes upon the crucified Christ on the rood, who is wounded as I am, is right. It is all I can do, but it never seems to be enough.

XX

One day Felicia reads me this prayer:

> Thou unbegun and everlasting Wisdom, the which in thyself
> art ... the Sovereign Goddess and the sovereign Good: ... I
> beseech thee to draw us up in an according ableness to where all
> privy things of divinity be covered and hid under the sovereign-
> shining darkness of wisest silence ...

The sovereign-shining darkness of wisest silence. I repeat these
words reverently, these strange exquisite words that resonate deeply
in me.

The prayer is Dionysius's. Soon after, Felicia reads further from his
same text, which she has been copying, *Hid Divinity*, glancing at me
from time to time as she reads, as the words turn everything I think
I know upside down and fill me with a strange relief:

> He hath no virtue, nor is He virtue, nor light, nor does He live,
> nor is He life, nor is He substance, nor age, nor time, nor is there
> any understandable touching of Him, nor is He cunning, nor
> truth, nor kingdom, nor wisdom, not one, not unity, not

Godheed, not goodness, nor is He spirit as we understand spirit, nor sonhead, nor fatherhead, nor any other thing known by us, nor of any that has been, nor is there any way by reason or understanding to come unto Him.

This is not what holy church teaches, I think, watching my mind's image of an angry God fade at the power of these new words.

Felicia says:

Do not try to make sense of this. Receive. The words' wisdom will work in you. The sovereign-shining darkness of wisest silence will work in you.

My mind is disconcerted by the gentle insistence of a truth beyond any imagining, but my heart is eased, and I do not know why.

The words fell on soft ground, Thomas, I see that now. How could I make sense of them when they directed me beyond all sense? Of course I could not. But they sounded in the darkness of my wounded, unhappy, uncertain, softened soul, and I did not resist them, and they sowed themselves deeply in me.

You are smiling. And so you should. For as we read texts together, the sisters and I, and we sought out good preaching from the Dominicans, Augustinians, Benedictines, Franciscans, any scholars who would share their learning with the laity, and the city was full of such; I discovered that Dionysius is no strange voice.

Darkness itself is the fullest illumination of the mind

declares a stooped Franciscan one Sunday afternoon, standing on a stone above the crowd gathered on the green outside the cathedral. His strong voice carries on the wind, clear and steady, and looking at him we are surprised at its power, for he is bent and frail and old, swallowed up in his rough brown habit and cloak, the skin of his bare sandalled feet like cracked old leather, toenails like thick horn.

We do not see the light, only that which is lit. We lie fallen in this sensible world, blind to the eternal truth, and we remain prostrate unless helped by truth itself in human form, Christ, whose rays of light descend into our minds. The irradiation and consideration of this light holds the wise suspended in wonder . . .

The sermon comes to an end and we walk slowly back to the community house, my mind hungry for contemplation of a God that is infinitely mysterious.

He was quoting Bonaventure, says Felicity.

The patron saint of bowel disorders, says Margaret.

The stooped Franciscan's open-ended teaching suits us. Many preachers present us with tidy arguments, neatly laid out and finished with a triumphant flourish of the intellect only. But these self-tutored lay women have learned by their own discernment to trust that God is infinite and that there will always be more to understand and even more beyond that which minds will never grasp. They are not afraid to ask questions to which there are no ready answers.

Over and over again my mind's certainties are loosened in this safe company of learners, and my heart is held. For four years, I am taught by the sisters and tended by my mother.

And I begin to wonder if the sisters' life might be where my future lies, if they would let me join them.

I wonder, but I do not say anything. I wait, because inside I do not cease to feel bruised and broken, lost, unworthy of their companionship, unable to receive love.

And then in 1373 I fall ill myself.

May 1373

XXI

Christ on the rood is blurring before my eyes. The whole cathedral seems to be swaying around me. Trying to stand steady in the nave, attending mass on the feast of St John of Beverley, I cannot hear the priest's words any more. I am suddenly shivering with cold. But now beads of sweat gather at the corners of my wimple and under my arms, and my mouth is dry, I cannot swallow. I grasp my mother's arm before I fall and she looks anxiously at me. Her face is enormous.

I can't breathe, I say.

And she gently but swiftly draws me away from the crowded nave to a side door and we leave. The cool air outside is a balm but I am barely able to walk.

We return slowly home to the cottage. By the time we have arrived I am in sore need, my mother placing a cold cloth on my brow as I sink into a chair by the hearth. Alice brings water, which I drink through a painfully swelling throat. Soon I can no longer sit and I withdraw with my mother's help to my bedchamber and climb gratefully into bed. It is the evening. I can eat no food and I fall into a troubled slumber, my dreams bright: I am with St John of Beverley and the Magdalene walking a long narrow winding path raised high above the fields, deep ditches either side, and they are striding ahead and I cannot keep up and I am swaying and the road lurches and the ditches are deep and I am falling now, falling . . . I waken, drenched in sweat. I force my trembling body up to wash and relieve itself and then I return, chilled through, to my bed, and eventually I sleep. The next day, the fever worsens. I feel with shaking fingers for the familiar swelling under my armpits and in my groin, but there is none. It is not the pestilence, but I feel as though life no longer wishes to live in me, and my soul is struggling to be free from my body, and I am not going to survive.

I linger for days in this liminal state, half conscious, feverish, dimly apprehending my mother's hand gently wiping my face and my neck and the murmured prayers of the women who quietly come and go; I see Felicia but then I think she is Matilda, there are other voices of people I do not know, and Alice and my mother clean me and freshen the bed and hold water to my lips, and I burn, and shake, and then a priest comes and I feel his light touch of oil on my forehead and my hands and I hear him say, in the power given to me I absolve you of all your sins – or I think I do – but now he is gone and I see Lora dancing and Martin laughing and a huge crucifix with saints chanting and devils gobbling around its base, and Lora is again in my arms, shaking and crying, and I waken to the call of my own voice, and then I sleep again, and now I see a great heap of bodies covered with sores of the pestilence crawling over each other and howling; and again I waken and so it goes on for days and days and I long for death and then in a shock of awakening my mind clears.

*

The room is completely dark.

I am propped up by pillows for ease of breathing and in the sudden fresh clarity of my mind I turn my thoughts and my eyes heavenward because I am going to die now.

My breath shortens. Death is slowly stealing upwards through my body, numb feet, numb legs, numb waist, numb everything but the laboured rising and falling of my chest and the gentle ache in my uplifted eyes.

My mother stirs in her chair by my bedside. I hear her murmur to Alice who steals out of the room. It is very quiet. I concentrate on looking upwards, waiting for my passing, but my eyes are beginning to hurt, and then the door opens and lets in some light and a small child. I wonder if I am dreaming again but a figure who is unmistakably our curate follows. Silently he comes to stand at the foot of my bed and the child passes him something and then he raises both arms towards me; he is holding up the thing the child passed him but my eyes are still fastened heavenwards.

Daughter, I have brought thee the image of thy Saviour. Look thereupon and comfort thee therewith.

Carefully and with relief I lower my eyes and fasten them on the crucifix held aloft in his gentle hands.

It glows in the shadows of the space between us. I do not know how it is lit.

And – it is bleeding.

Not painted-on blood, but freshly bleeding, as though Christ himself is there in his body, and the crown of thorns has just been rammed onto his head, cutting into the forehead, the red blood running down his face in great gobs.

Am I dreaming? My mind remains crystal clear and I am wide awake, but I do not believe what I see, not at first, Thomas. I have not seen such strangeness before. Others speak of statues moving or weeping or bleeding; the pilgrim who visited us saw the holy Vernicle smile. But I have never seen such things. Never.

But the crucifix is glowing in its own light and I can see it clearly and my Lord is bleeding.

I cease to question and simply watch.

And now in the light shed by the cross I see a young woman barely out of childhood. Her eyes are fixed on me, but I do not think she sees me. Her lips are parted in an astonished O and her eyes – in her eyes I see intense concentration, and fear, or is it awe?

I understand in my heart that this is Mary as she was when she conceived. And she is . . . even now . . . receiving God into her body.

I see her again, Thomas, as I speak to you, and she is looking into my eyes and I can feel in my body the dread that she felt and I understand it better because the visions came to birth in me and they too are so much greater than I. In her conceiving of God, Mary was a poor creature of no consequence, as am I.

Why does God come to such as we? I have so often wondered. It is why I wanted to speak my story to you.

Is it because we know we are nothing?

Out of nothing, something is coming to birth.

Seeing Mary receive the Creator of the universe into her own body breaks open my own being to receive what is to come, not just to witness but to receive into the heart of me all its strangeness and size. To be transformed as Mary is transformed by her receiving.

*

The crucifix is still bleeding. I see Mary no more but now I feel a mantle of the softest cloth, so fine but so strong it will last for ever, wrap itself about my shoulders and my body, enclosing me as a child is swaddled to know that though born it is still protected: my bruised child's soul is comforted at last. Comforted. I am wrapped about and protected and safe, ready to receive more of this great seeing that is coming to birth within me.

And then I feel a light brushing on my palm, like a breath, and I look at the place where I feel this lightness and it is the whole universe, everything that is made, and it is round, and tiny, the size of a hazelnut, shelled and unprotected, almost not there, utterly vulnerable, and it is everything. It is an all-fragile thing held only by the love that enfolds me without and pulses within.

Not God's will, Thomas. Not by God's will is this fragile world held. By God's love.

And I speak out of the love that is being born so enormous within me and the warm protecting love that is so enfolding about me, and between the two I am disappearing, almost not there, and I say:

I am dying!

My second childhood wish comes to pass.

I am, now, truly at the doorway of death, pressed to nothing between the love within and the love without. But the face of Christ before me is still bleeding, blood pouring out from within him and now there are spit and spite and blows raining upon him from without, though I cannot see the fiends who do this to him. He is bleeding terrible pain within and he is enfolded in hatred without. He too is at the doorway of death, pressed to nothing between the pain within and the pain without.

I do not understand the pain and the love. I need more light, to see more clearly, but there is no light in me nor in the room, only the crucifix shines in the darkness; only from itself will I understand the pain and the love. This thing of pain and love that is being born is its own truth and nothing can explain it except itself. There is only this light. I am at the doorway of death and all I see is Jesu, crucified, alight.

XXII

The light shows this: all that is made, God makes it. All that is, God makes. I see this, Thomas. I see it! All things in God and God in a point, single, only.

And God is not angry, God is good, this is good, this is all good, but the blood is still pouring from Christ's body in a great flood, the pain pouring out of him. What does it mean? There is so much blood I think it will soak the bed and keep falling and flowing till it has flooded the world. Still the only light is the crucifix and still the only place is the point where God is, and yet there is all this blood. What does it mean?

And now a voice speaks in me:

Herewith is the fiend overcome.

And in the blood and the spit and the spite raining from and upon Jesu, and in the now-returned sharp pain of my illness in my body and the pain of my guilt in my heart, I feel the malice of the fiend and I see that the fiend is all the evil there is: not I but the fiend lodged in my heart; not the men beating upon Jesu but the fiend besetting him;

not the people on whom the pestilence has fallen who carry the blame for it but the fiend, a thing dense with malice, compacted with hate, doling out blame – that is where all the evil is and it feels so strong but I feel the scorn of God and then I see the fiend is made unmighty by its own hatred, its hatred makes it weak not strong, and I laugh at the fiend

but Christ does not laugh

and I see the fiend-evil may be weak but I have made it strong by my unknowing, we have all made it strong by our unknowing, and we do not have the wherewithal to undo our unknowing; only Christ's pain will free our bonds, only Christ's pain will overcome the fiend-evil.

Christ's pain.

Christ's pain is love. Love.

It is unbearable.

This is the love that holds the universe?

And now my bodily pain recedes as I am shown a great hall full of people sitting at long tables laden with fruit of every kind glowing fresh and ripe and goblets of ruby-rich mead and they laugh together and sing and speak and it is heaven and God does not sit at the great high seat but moves among them, speaking to one and then another, and God is thanking them. And now I am seated among them, drinking from a golden cup, and God approaches and speaks to me:

I thank thee for thy service and thy travail, especially in thy youth.

A clutching knot of anxiety inside me softens as I receive gratitude for efforts I had called failures: my fearful helpless watch at my dying father's bedchamber, my vain struggles to keep my vows of contrition and compassion and especially longing for an angry God I did not love, my hard unfruitful work to appease that invented God, my poor efforts to fulfil a householder's duties, my reluctant return to a home I had fled and my too-late tending of a dead husband and a dying daughter. Tight anxiety at failure softened by the recognition of . . . effort. Just that.

I watch God move on, thanking soul after soul for their travail, not their triumph. I watch him with grateful love in my heart.

The vision departs and I come to myself in my bed, utterly at ease. My heart is peaceful, held in soft love, troubled by nothing. My body rests. I am grateful and happy and loving and beloved.

And in a flash I am again filled with anxious care and now I am furious with everything. My body is hot, shifting restlessly in the bed, sweating and in pain. I feel no love of God nor of my fellows. My mother fusses over me and I am cross with her. The curate's eyes upon me are more visible to me than the crucifix he is holding and I am irritated with him. Alice is crashing about the room doing nothing that matters. The whole world is enraged and I am swimming in its misfortune, helpless to serve and lacking any will to do so.

And just as I begin to wonder how such peace could turn into such discomfort in so little time, the peace returns and I am as easy and contented as before. Thank God, I cry inwardly, the woe has passed and I feel Your love again, and I am in love with those in the room and all that they are so carefully doing for me, and I could lie here quietly for ever. The woe was a moment that passed, leaving nothing behind. It was nothing.

But the peace is gone again without warning and back comes the sweaty irritation and discomfort. Where does this come from? I had no time to do wrong and deserve it. And it passes again, swept back like a heavy curtain drawn by an unseen hand, and the lovely soft and kindly peace returns and I reflect that I had no time to deserve the peace either. Back and forth, back and forth I go from peace to perturbation, again and again, till I understand deep in my soul, deeper than either feeling, that this is the way of things and I should be patient with the pain when it comes and enjoy the peace when it comes. This is the way of it. And I see in my life thus far great swings from peace to pain and I am glad that I have endured whatever I have felt. This is the way of it, Thomas, and how much more I see this after so many more years of weal and woe, weal and woe, in my heart, in this anchorhold, in the words spoken by those who seek my counsel, in the world of pestilence and war and persecution and beauty and love.

Enter and endure, do not deny, the pain.

Admit the love.

So what, Thomas, of the pestilence? Is it God's wrath? I am shown it is not.

Enter and endure the pain and it will, it *will* transform. Herewith, here, by this entering and enduring, is the fiend overcome.

XXIII

The blood has dried. Christ on the curate's crucifix is dying before me. His face and all his body are brown like tanned leather, the rents in his skin from the thorns and the nails hang loosely, stirred by a cold wind, he is hung out to dry in the cold wind, he is drying up before me and now he looks straight at me out of his face twisted in pain and he cries:

I thirst!

And then, Thomas, right then, in that beseeching call for respite out of helpless suffering, in his appeal to me so directly, as though I were the power and he the powerless, as though only I can quench his thirst, right then: my heart melts and I fall in love with Jesu.

But my love is too late, I cannot bring him water, I cannot save him, and now my heart is breaking to watch my beloved in pain from thirst within and rent flesh dried by cold wind without: he is drying up, shrivelling and slowly dying, so slowly it feels as though days are passing and he is in so much pain but still he does not die. My heart is breaking to watch my beloved suffer, impotent by his side, again the soul-tearing impotence of a mother by my dying child Lora, and as I did then I cry out with all that I am: let me take this pain in myself!

And I do.

My first childhood wish is granted. Instantly I cry out for it to stop. This is not discomfort. This is the pain of the moment of Lora being born, the unbearable pain, the unspeakably intense pain of my body riven apart and the piercing sharp fierce fire through all my body and beyond, there is nothing beyond the pain, but with Lora's birth it came quickly to pass and this does not, and I beg for the pain to be taken away but it does not pass, and I shout:

Is this pain the worst that ever there was?

No.

No?

Spoken from the dry lips of Christ before me

No. Hell is worse. For in hell there is despair.

I have seen despair in others and I have felt it too, Thomas, holding me in its dreary vice after Lora died. It is empty. There is nothing to draw you out of the vast emptiness that has no end, you feel nothing, not even fear; there is no joy and no hope of joy; there is no meaning in your pain but there is pain, dull pain, and it will go nowhere; it will not pass like the curtain drawn back; it is dead, listless, pointless; there is no air, no light; the world is misty with unshed tears and so are your own dead eyes; you are alone with no energy, no hope.

Everything in you is stillborn, useless; nothing you are or have done has any worth; you have a weight on your chest so great you can hardly move; a feeling like a snake in you writhing. Your limbs are slack. You care about nothing least of all yourself. Hopeless. Barren. That is despair.

This pain, this pain of the cross, is sharp and true and it is bringing love to birth in me, but even as I gaze on my cold, drying, dying brother and am entirely one with him in his pain, a hand lays itself on my face and tries to close my eyes:

My mother! She thinks I am dead.

And now a silky persuading voice, not hers, speaks to me:

Look away from the cross, look up to heaven, where the happy people eat and drink and God thanks them and there is no more pain.

This is heaven.

I speak with a whisper that feels like thunder. The silky voice is silent and my mother withdraws her startled hand as my eyes refuse to close, they refuse to abandon their steadfast watch upon the crucifix, keeping the pain alive in me even as it is killing my brother. I choose this: I *choose* this as heaven, this sharp truthful pain of love which is the way to love, and as I do so and my brother Jesu is still dying, still hanging there like a cloth blown in the cold, cold wind, I see Mary and John and the Magdalene at the foot of the rood, they who love him also and are as helpless to take away his suffering, they are shaking in pain that is just as great; and now the planets and the elements and the whole universe is cramped and crunched up in flinching fear and howling loss and there is no goodness or hope or light anywhere, and this horrific screaming tearing desolation passes in a moment, a blink and it is the end, but I do not see Jesu die.

I must draw breath, Thomas. I will tell more, but leave me now to rest, here at the foot of the cross, with Christ's lovers.

XXIV

I t is the end but I do not see Jesu die.

Like a clear ray of light comes new life. It has passed through the pain and the pain is dissolved to nothing and his ravaged face smiles.

It is as though a child has been born.

Daylight floods into the room as Alice draws the curtain and light fills me within and without as I keep my gaze fixed upon my beloved.

I did not see Jesu die. The shrieking pain has passed but he has gone nowhere, he hangs there still, his smiling ravaged face ugly like the image on the Vernicle the pilgrim described all those years ago. He hangs there still on the rood that would kill him, his body torn and buffeted by the cold wind and the dryness and the nails and the blows of his tormentors, but he is smiling now, he is newborn.

There are murmurs around me as the room is tidied and my mother carefully washes my face and smooths my hair and Alice straightens the bedclothes, but the curate remains stock still and my eyes do not leave my brother on the cross, my brother who is asking me a question in a gentle persistent voice:

My darling. Art thou well apaid?

Art thou well apaid? Am *I* satisfied?

Is it not God who is to be satisfied?

And now, in me, in a moment, rises fury, an unstoppable wave rearing up and crashing into every part of me, fury not with myself, not with Martin, but with God! With God, for visiting upon a helpless people such a foul, terrifying pestilence that has all but destroyed us. Everything in me is turned on its head as I find it is not I who needs to be forgiven.

I need to forgive God.

My darling, art thou well apaid?

I look through angry tears at my beloved Jesu, torn and battered, showing all the signs still of the pain through which he has passed, pain which still resonates in my own body.

My darling, art thou well apaid?

And the crashing wave of fury shivers, settles, and withdraws as I receive and accept the sacrifice, the expiation, the atonement. For all that we have suffered. God in Jesu has put Himself where we are and His pain is our pain. I marvel at it.

Art thou well apaid?

Yes, Lord, I whisper, and then—

If I could have suffered more, I would have suffered more, says God.

No more! I am content!

And the fury is gone and I receive Jesu, Jesu whose eyes are full of laughing love, reaching into my porous self, and rich joy, new life uncurls in me like a baby fern and as it grows, the fury and the fear and the pain like weaker weeds lose their strength and the softened anxious knot in me dissolves altogether as I myself accept and forgive that frightened child who ran away from her father and that pent-up matron who ran away from her husband and child, I myself accept and forgive the God who let the pestilence happen, and now my darling brother Christ, my darling mother Christ, highest joy and dreadful mighty power, has paid the price of love – love, Thomas, not wrath – which is pain, pain I have touchèd, the terrible pain of love; it is costly but it is not a debt, it is gratitude, there is no contract just an invitation. So I grow, Thomas, I grow uncurling and unfurling inside and open my arms outside to receive this rich joy and I am dissolving in love and I am smiling too and warmth passes through my body and life wants to live and energy rises and anything is possible and nothing has come to an end, nothing, only the rich joy is released and who knows what will happen or what it might serve in the world's weal and woe, for there will be woe but it is apaid and the rich joy is released like tasty food to a hungry stomach or a blazing fire to a cold body or a strong embrace to a lonely soul or deep rest to a troubled mind or the sudden cessation of pain. And I receive and I grow to receive more as more is offered and I will accept the love to keep it flowing and growing, this rich joy:

My dear darling. Art thou well apaid?

Tears spill from me.

Yea, Lord, gramercy.

*

Thomas, I need to rest again. I did not know you would draw such words from me.

XXV

I am restored and can speak some more. Yesterday you rose on the instant that I asked and left without a word or question, left me in my own peace. For this I love you more than I can say.

After you had gone I turned to my altar and knelt on my old knees in the rushes and was lost in contemplating my beloved Lord. No more words. It is very simple. And the energy that had gone from me with the passion of my words to you was quietly restored as my mind softened and my heart opened and my body rested and quiet contentment suffused me. And I slept, Thomas, better than I have done for some time.

*

Rich joy continues to unfurl and grow in me as my gaze remains fastened on my beloved who is laughing merrily, whose face shines even as he hangs there still on the cross, still broken, still wounded, his shining face still Vernicle-ugly.

He is still wounded. He is risen and he is still wounded.

As I gaze on him, the wound in his side opens wide and I find myself entering the gaping space, large enough to receive me and large enough to receive every creature. I move through halls hung with softness, gently led, and I see Jesu standing in simplicity, welcoming me and every soul and saying my darling, my dear darling, how I love thee. Let me show how much I love thee. Look, here is my mother: see how I love her? That is how much I love thee.

In that great space opened to me and to all of us through his wounds, deep now in the heart of Jesu, I see Mary three times: as a young woman when she conceived her son, and in deepest sorrow at the cross, and in a blaze of glory as the queen of heaven, enthroned, crowned, bright-faced, and then the brightness of her face grows till it is her face no longer and I see God! In glory, for a moment, and the greatest joy beyond imagining fills me until there is only joy, or is it love and it is such a relief, Thomas. A relief to see and to feel and to know that God is mother-love and love is true.

Why do I not see this all the time? What blinds me to such brightness?

Sin.

I flinch. I do not want to hear this word. I do not want the knot of self-blame to be tied again around my heart. But I feel myself in God's motherly regard, the mother who has suffered more than words or imagination can conjure, whom I have forgiven, and the love is still all that He is and the knot does not return. So I ask

What, then, is sin? And why is it?

God says:

Sin is behovely. But all shall be well. You will see that all shall be well. You will understand.

I am not satisfied with promises. I want to understand now.

Why is there sin and what is it if I do not see it in Thee?

And that is when I see the fall of Adam but it is so strange.

I see a lord seated and a man standing before him. They gaze at each other with eyes so full of love it is as a tangible thing between them. Then the lord stirs and speaks to the man, who turns and runs fast to do his lord's bidding but in his haste on the narrow path he trips and falls into the deep ditch by the side of the path. I see him lying there with his body bruised and broken, his face covered in cuts and worst of all his head facing away from his lord. So he cannot see that his lord is still gazing upon him with love that melts my heart.

And the two characters are the same as those I saw in the pageant all those years ago, the one just after the pestilence had left us for the first time, I a child. The lord has the face of God and the man has the face of Adam. Only I do not see Eve and there is no snake and no apple and no angry God punishing.

This is what I see. I do not understand it. I do not see sin and blame, only hurry and falling and bruising and blindness. It seems dangerous, heretical, what I see. This I feel: that God in this showing has answered my question about sin. And this I understand: that the tripping and the falling are the greatest harm, they are the sin, and there is no fault, and God holds it in compassion and God has made it well. And that is what I told you at the time, Thomas.

It was not until many years had passed that greater understanding came and I could see more of this showing, much more, and then I saw much more in all the other showings, and I had to start again to write what I saw because my understanding had grown. But all that comes much later.

*

The pageant picture fades from my inward sight leaving me in utter peace. I am filled with such a strong desire to die now, because I know that the peace will pass and the woe will return, frail human that I am, and I do not think my body has the strength to face any more pain. And then God speaks in my heart:

Suddenly thou shalt be taken.

And I am shown a man's body lying in murk and filth, and a child's body rising up from the filth, entirely clean, and God says:

Be patient. Suffer a little while, this weal and woe is no more than a point, it is nothing. I will make all things well; I shall make all things well; I may make all things well; I can make all things well; thou shalt see for thyself that all manner of things shall be well.

And self-hatred, which I have worn like a skin against my body, so close I did not know it was there, sloughs off me. It is the deepest cleansing I have ever had and as it peels away from me I feel raw and new and simple and weak.

I sleep for many hours.

XXVI

When I awaken, the curate has gone and sitting by me is a round comfortable figure in a Benedictine habit, his hands resting on his stomach, his kind, as-yet-unlined face bent upon me with a steady gaze.

You! Dear Thomas. How is it that you came and no other? I had not seen you before, you were simply there in answer to a call from my mother to the cathedral community that a religious person should attend to her daughter if she died or if she wakened from her sleep. It could have been any from your monastery.

Still drowsy, I say, laughing at myself:

I raved today. I thought the crucifix bled.

You do not laugh.

You do not laugh.

You will not dismiss my visions. And so I do not dismiss them either.

I was shocked then and I am still shocked at how easily I could have rejected them, had you not looked so serious. Would another priest have laughed at me? I do not know. I was ill, I had been delirious, my truth as a woman was not trusted, and there was much madness abroad from the pestilence and all its woes. He may have laughed. But you did not.

You leave me to rest with a promise to return.

In peace I lie quietly in my bed as my mother and Alice tend to my body and change the linen and make all well. I feel strength return. I swallow a little broth.

And then a terrible stink invades the room and the face of the fiend hovers over my bed, staring down at me, gobbling and gabbling like arguing voices, and smoke billows around me and I cry out,

Is the room on fire?

But my mother says it is not and tries to calm me and as her hand touches my brow I feel my beloved mother Jesu enter my soul and entirely fill it till there is no room and he and I are one. The fiend vanishes, the smoke blows away, the stink slowly recedes, and God says:

Reflect on all you have seen for all that you need is held therein.

You shall not be overcome.

He did not say, you shall not be tempested. He did not say you shall not be travailed and He did not say you shall not be diseased. He said:

You shall not be overcome.

Once more peace descends and I rest until night falls again and I sleep through the night and I know that my body is returning to health and that I have work to do.

XXVII

The next day you reappear, Thomas, and ask me to tell you of my showings and I open my mouth and speak all that has happened, all that I have seen, my wonder at what I have seen, my hope that the visions will speak directly to my fellow Christians. And as I speak I see how the visions came out of the wounds I asked for as a child so I tell you of these. I speak to you for three days as fully as I can remember in my still-weak state and you write everything down and on the fourth day you stay away. You return only from time to time over the next weeks, checking your notes with me, ensuring accuracy, and a month after my visions you return with your writing completed. You say,

These words, these simple English words which I have written at your dictation, they should be read by others.

Here is how I begin, just as you spoke to me:

I desired three graces by the gift of God. The first was to have mind of Christ's passion. The second was bodily sickness, and the third was to have of God's gift three wounds . . .

And you go on reading to me, and you have written my words truly and well. I am glad that you include this:

> God showed me full great pleasance that He has in all men and women that mightily and meekly and worshipfully take the preaching and the teaching of holy church, for He is holy church . . .

for I do not want my words to turn people from holy church.

You do not write that I have forgiven God.

I ask you to write this, not wanting anyone to understand from the words that the showings are just for me:

> I pray you all for God's sake, and counsel you for your own profit that ye leave the beholding of the wretched worm, sinful creature that it was showed unto, and that ye mightily, wisely, lovingly and meekly behold God, who of His courteous love and His endless goodness would show generally this vision in comfort of us all . . . for it is common and general as we are all one and I am sure I saw it for the profit of many others.

And, far-seeing Thomas, you end the script leaving my mind's door wide open for more to be said, as though you know, you know only too well, how much more there will be to say:

> All the blessed teaching of our Lord God was showed to me by three parts, that is to say by the bodily sight, and by word formed in mine understanding, and by ghostly sight. For the bodily sight, I have said as I saw, as truly as I can. And for the words formed, I have said them right as our Lord showed me them. And for the

ghostly sight, I have said some deal, but I may never fully tell it; and therefore of this ghostly sight I am stirred to say more, as God will give me grace.

*

The writing is copied and shared. I am content with this. I think the words will not be read by many, because they are from a woman. And for those who do read, I have claimed no role of teacher and I have urged my readers to follow holy church in all things. The words are cautious. And at such a time, it is not thought dangerous to write in English. Greater clarity of what the showings mean, and greater danger, are yet to come.

1373—1377

XXVIII

I regain my health and all around me the country is coming back to life too, slowly and painfully, after the sore trial of the latest wave of the pestilence. John visits, proudly showing me his son, Edward, and his wife Alba, whom he married within a year of my departure. Her belly swells again, and John is happy. He has found new apprentices and labourers in a sparse population by paying and treating them well and he has resumed merchanting with a vengeance.

My body is healthy but I am changed. Everything is changed. I have walked through death and I no longer fear it. I watch young Edward, who has learned to call me aunt, prance on a broomstick he has turned into a horse, and I cannot but laugh at his antics, even as I am reminded of Lora and think that she would be eleven years of age now, but the memory is gentle. I feel how my harsh guilty loss and pain for my daughter, my husband and my father really have passed from me, leaving a soft grief that I know will never leave, but which I can abide. I am grateful for it: it will keep me gentle with others, gentle on myself.

I tell you, Thomas, the grief does indeed never leave, and even now it can return charged with pain, unexpectedly provoking a storm of tears or a deep woeful quiet. It returns and it passes. In the time it is with me, I have learned that I should turn fully towards those I have lost, and mourn them and honour them afresh.

In the solar now with Edward playing on his hobby horse, a great depth of stillness sits within me that feels both unassailable and porous, like a still lake with easy banks for everyone to sit by, to drink from, to see their faces reflected, to bathe in. Edward stops his prancing and comes and leans against my knee, looking up at me. He does not speak but puts his finger to my cheek to feel the wetness there.

*

I stay with my mother, feeling no pressure to decide anything, trusting that what comes next will be shown. The visions are my companions and I let them mull in me, like compost from which new life will come, slowly turning and reforming and presenting themselves, a good intelligent loving challenging friend whose deepness calls to my deep.

I speak of them with you when you visit, and soon with others, for now people come and find me. Your manuscript of my words has reached them and they want to ask me about the visions and seek my advice. I respond sparingly. I am not wise, I tell them. I saw these things. Read and see what they show you. Do not look at me, look at your beloved Saviour Jesu.

I return to the sisters on Elm Hill, not from dawn to dusk as before, but still frequently. I no longer help with the parchmenting, my efforts have never amounted to much and I think Margaret is relieved. But I go out in the afternoons to care for the poor, and I go with the sisters to hear good preaching, and I stay in the evenings to read and converse.

I tell Felicia of my visions. She listens with her characteristic deep openness and she does not try to make sense of them. She sees how new they are, how much in them there is to understand, and she knows it will take time. Instead of questioning me, she encourages me to start copying some texts.

This will continue to feed your soul, she says, like the visions have. It will help keep them alive to you.

And I discover how this simple act is as prayer, as I carefully scribe words that enter my soul deeply. I copy Dionysius's prayer and some chapters from his book. I copy the words:

nor is there any way by reason or understanding to come unto Him

and as my pen moves slowly, marking the letters of the words, the very place where my pen touches the page, nay, finer than that, the ink at the tip of my nib touching the page, that place becomes so enormous, Thomas, and so still, my eyes and all my attention rest there in that point and I draw down deep within and my soul swells beyond any thought or reason or understanding, it swells with God-love, God-energy and I emerge from my copying as one who has encountered God, profoundly refreshed, more deeply fed and rested than any food or soft bed could afford.

I copy from another book that Felicia loves, *The Cloud of Unknowing*, written by a Carthusian monk who has remained anonymous:

Pierce the cloud with thy sharp dart of longing love, and go not hence for thing that befalleth

and my pen is the dart and the ink my love and I do not wish to go anywhere away from here, from this quiet beseeching, from this deep trusting, from this nourishing food that makes no sense.

Together we read the arguments in *The Cloud of Unknowing* in favour of Mary the sister of Martha, and we argue amongst ourselves.

The story told in the Gospel is perfectly clear, insists Felicia. Jesu visits the sisters, Mary who sits at his feet listening to his words, and Martha who cooks. When Martha complains that Mary has left all the work to her, he tells her she is worried about many things and she should leave Mary alone, for Mary has chosen the one thing that is needed, and it is good. That is what *The Cloud* is saying: the contemplative life is good, it is needed more than anything else, only those who are active do not understand.

And *I* don't understand, says Berta. For how can the world be cared for if we all sit around doing nothing?

It's not nothing, says Felicia, her eyes flashing. Contemplation is hard work, lonely, needing concentration and quiet.

It will not feed the widows

But it will open our hearts to God's love

Still, it will not feed the widows. Berta is adamant.

Nor will it feed us, says Margaret. We would not be able to live as we do if we were not active parchmenters.

I listen to the argument flow. It is one I have heard the sisters have before, as they try to balance good works and prayer and earning the living upon which they all depend. I do not think there is an easy answer, but as I listen this evening I recognise that for me, there is no food that refreshes as much as prayer does. Margaret is energised by her hard physical work on the parchment hides; Berta returns from her widows with a light step and a smile on her face; I am exhausted by both. But like Felicia and unlike them I could sit and copy, or quietly contemplate my visions, for hours.

I am waiting for something to become clear in my own mind and heart. I want to be of service. I want the visions to speak through me to the world. To speak of love. But does that love show in deeds only? If also through silent prayer, how?

XXIX

Yet another wave of the pestilence passes through our land. There is a dull hopeless sluggish unhappy endurance in the people, enslaved to loss with no prospect of freedom. The sisters and I tend to them when and where we can. And for a time Martha's labours are favoured above Mary's contemplation, to meet their urgent need. It is necessary, and exhausting.

*

And then, on a cold autumn night in 1375, my beloved mother dies, quietly, not from the pestilence but in calm old age, in her sleep. I mourn her and I miss her but I am not sorry to see her pass. Her body was failing, she could no longer see nor hear well, she could not be as active as she wished, and she was tired.

Alice is inconsolable for a while, for my mother was as a mother to her. She had been brought into the embrace of our family when she was a child and my mother taught her everything she knows, including her letters. We stand before each other, sadness for our loss flowing between us as sisters. The woman Alice has grown into is strong and vital, taller than I by a head and broader; she is like an oak while I am like a birch, I think, or a willow, thin from my illness and slight, my long mousy hair and hazel eyes contrasting with the thick unruly waves of her black hair tucked into her cap and her black-browed shrewd green eyes.

I know that Alice has family some distance from Norwich, and could return to them.

Will you stay? I ask.

I will, she says. This is my home, you are my family, and you need me.

She is right. With her steady service I can continue to live in the cottage on my own. And the landowner is content for me to stay, as he was my mother, and I have John's pension. I am steady and confident in my quiet life, spending time on my own each day reflecting on the visions, and with Alice I tend the vegetable plot and the sheep and goats and hens. I go often to Elm Hill. And your manuscript is abroad, Thomas, and being copied, and more visitors come seeking me.

XXX

Receiving visitors. It is service of a kind, though I do not think it matches the active charity of the sisters.

Then one hot afternoon in the summer, kneeling in my garden, I hear horses approaching. I stand, brushing the dusty earth from my skirt, and watch a great lady and her escort ride up to my cottage. She dismounts with swift elegance, the cloak-buckle at her throat flashing silver in the sunlight.

Leave us. Her tone is commanding.

The men take the horses and their noise elsewhere, and she turns to me, and in a much softer voice she says

I am Isabel, Countess of Suffolk. May I speak with you?

I curtsey low and she raises me.

Please, she says, would you call me Isabel? And would you give me mead to drink?

I bring her in to the solar where Alice quietly serves us and we sit together as equals, in silence for a while. Taught by the lay sisters, I do not fuss over her as a host or worry that she is not comfortable but let the silence be easy.

I sought you, Isabel begins, finally. I sought you because I read your account of your visions and they spoke to me. I am new to the study of theology and a novice in the things of God but your words made sense. That is, I understand them, and I want to believe them, to believe that all shall be well, Julian, but . . .

her voice trails away, and then she speaks in a great rush.

How can all be well, when there is so much pain and loss in the world?

Her eyes are blazing suddenly.

Here am I, she says, a great lady, no doubt my wealth is envied, I have a husband I am lucky enough to love but . . . He is my second husband. And I am still childless.

I murmur, but she waves my sympathy away.

Do not weep for that. Of course I would be sorry for my childlessness, for nobility needs no barren wives, and my husband William is only the second Earl. He was nervous of the title being lost from his family, but there are plenty of healthy nephews now. He loves me and he does not blame me for being barren.

She suddenly starts to her feet and paces in front of the fireplace.

But I am *not barren*. I have fallen pregnant many times, but every time, *every single time*, I have miscarried my child. Again and again my womb has rejected the new life in me.

I still remember the pain of the first babe coming loose in me, bleeding away my life, bleeding away my heart.

She takes her seat again and her words come more slowly.

Can you shriek in silence? I did. And I walked as one dead inside, my poor unconsoled empty body moving through the days and weeks and I all the time shrieking, shrieking inside.

And the pain when it happened again was worse. Each time, the pain of loss was no less.

I mourn each unformed child. They came away too soon to be acknowledged by the priest and there are no graves in the ground but I have thirteen graves in my heart, Julian, and I visit them every day and still weep bitter tears for their lives that never were.

More tears fall.

I told neither husband of my daily mourning. Till now I have not told anyone how real my unformed children are to me. I am ashamed of my feelings, a selfish not-mother hugging my not-babes to myself when so many mothers have lost children to the pestilence, children who were born and could be seen and loved. I am strange, am I not? My children were never born, I never knew them, they are almost not there at all. But they are *here*,

and Isabel places her hand at her breast,

and *here*,

and she places her hand on her belly.

And then, impatiently, she dashes the tears from her eyes.

I have so much for which I should be grateful! I relish my free-dom. I love to exercise in the fresh air, however bleak or warm the weather; I hunt and practise archery; and I also love to return to my room and read and reflect, ordering copies to be made of texts so I can study them, and I heard of yours and ordered that too. When I read it I had so many questions about sin and damnation and God's wrath and God's love and I wanted to talk to you, so I have come to see you, but as we sit together now it is only this terrible emptiness that is in me, not theology.

I did not think I would speak so.

I cannot find my way past my loss, she says.

I listen. I receive her words and I have none of my own. I feel like a sponge, absorbing not just Isabel's words but the hot pain that sits inside them, a pain that stays hidden from the world and is intense from its suppression. As the words and the pain enter me, enter my heart and, it feels, my whole body, even as a part of me is wondering at what is happening and fearful for myself, the pain is so hot, and for my lack of words of comfort, I trust that this is how it is and must be, and that it is not I who can determine how to receive and relieve the pain, but Jesu, Love herself, and I must allow this soft porosity to open to the healing love that is waiting to serve. So I sit quieter still, wondering and trusting and unknowing.

Isabel begins again to speak.

I have names for each of my unformed children. How could I know if they were boys or girls? But I felt I knew and I named each one.

May I tell you their names?

I say, not knowing where the thought has come from,

Yes, speak their names and we will together acknowledge them, love them, mourn them, and commit them to God. Lay them to rest.

And Isabel tells them. Her voice trembles as she speaks. It is not easy to say these names that have not before been said out loud. This is holy ground, where the names are spoken. It seems to me that as each name is called out, a child appears between us and before God, shines, is seen, just for a moment, and then lies down and sleeps.

Isabella. John. Margaret. Beatrice. Emma. Ralph. William. Matilda. Walter. Mabel. Roger. Hugh. Cecilia.

We remain silent for a long time. In the silence, in my body at least, the pain cools and melts away. A great stillness grows which is full of tenderness for all grieving mothers. This is what I feel.

And then I ask Isabel how she fares, for I do not know whether this was a comfort to her or not. Her strong, steady smile and the light in her eyes tell me she is well. She says:

> I feel so relieved. At last I have properly acknowledged my children, and now I can leave them in God's care. I cannot thank you enough.

She hesitates.

> Where . . .?

I know she is asking if they are in heaven and, Thomas, I do not know the answer to this. They are unformed, they could not be baptised, some scholars would even say they had no soul. But I do not think that theology can tell us who or where they are. I do know this, truly, that they are enfolded in love, and they are well. And I softly say that, and Isabel is satisfied.

She rises and grasps my hands in hers.

> Thank you.

And before I have time to do more than rise myself, she has turned and left my home. I hear her calling her entourage, and stand at my door to see her ride away, head held imperiously, back straight and supple on her horse, noble, light, free.

I stay still in the doorway and breathe the air gratefully. I am trembling a little and feel strangely weak and empty. I am not sure what has happened but I think: it is good.

Alice seems to understand. She brings me carefully to the table and gives me milk and cooks some eggs with herbs, and I drink and eat, and my strength returns.

XXXI

And so, Thomas, I begin to learn how to allow the love the showings birthed in me to heal another. And I begin to see that this is my service, this is my way to help a grieving world. I feel I know nothing, but I trust that it is not I who knows what a person needs, but Love. I only listen, receive, and in the listening the person's words themselves become the means of healing, not my words, or only rarely. I do almost nothing, but my attentive holding of the other, my entire absorption in the other, leaves me drained for a time.

That first encounter with Isabel, who becomes my good friend, helps me to hear the calling to the life of an anchoress, though I did not know what that was, then.

But so does this encounter.

A year from my mother's death, when winter is biting at the heels of autumn, stripping the trees bare in sudden, hungry gusts of wind and shocks of rain, when the cold creeps under the door and has me banking up the warm fire in my hearth, two men arrive seeking admittance. They are peasants but their clothes are of good russet wool and they are not starved, though they are grateful for the weak ale I offer and Alice brings to them, and the bread and cheese and cooked onion. The older man, too thin for his height, names himself Adam and his broad-shouldered companion William. They sit at my table and eat, quietly not roughly, every now and then stealing a glance at me. They are a gentle presence and I am not afraid. I work at my sewing, to give my hands something to do and my eyes somewhere to rest, to give them space to find their own peace.

When they have finished eating and I have removed their bowls and cups and seated myself again, my hands folded in my lap, my eyes upon them, William speaks.

We have come because of your words.

He stops for a moment, as though he is struggling to say what he needs. Now there is a repressed excitement in him which grows as he speaks, and I do not trust it.

Your words. They are full of the love of Jesu; you had a powerful experience, mistress. You were shown truth. And we . . . we know truth; we know it more clearly and simply than it is told to us by the priests. They complicate God with their Latin. They tell us what is in scripture and we have no way to see for ourselves. They tell us to pray to wood and plaster and stone and bread and wine, not to the living God and His Son. They tell us when our sins are forgiven, that we can walk to where the dead saints are, and our pilgrimages and our money will buy our way to heaven.

There is a fleck of spittle at the corner of William's mouth. Adam sits bolt-silent and still, watching me as William's words pour forth. The words are terrible to me because they are true and not true at the same time, clouding and confusing my mind. He continues:

> And who are our priests? Are they holy men? They are not. They own land, they fight wars, they are corrupted by the world. They are not like Christ. What lands did he rule? What war did he fight? He rejected the world while our priests make themselves lords of it. And they are corrupted by their very vows of celibacy which make them mad with lust—

> Cease this! I cry, holding my hands to my ears.

William looks contrite.

> I did not mean to offend, sister. But – you know of what I am speaking.

I take my hands from my ears and stare at this honest troubled man who seeks no counsel but wants my soul.

> You are one of us.

Now I do not understand what he means. He goes on:

> You placed the secret message in your words.

> What?

> In your words.

William is nodding his head, his voice emphatic. A cold chill clutches at my heart. What have I done?

William pulls a well-worn parchment sheaf from his tunic and lays it on the table. I recognise that it is a copy of your script, Thomas. He searches feverishly, his stubby finger moving down the lines of writing. It has been badly copied and the words are hard to distinguish.

Here.

He points, his finger pressing into the parchment, to a line, and reads:

Each soul after the saying of Saint Paul *should feel in him that in Christ Jesu.*

Sister, you hid these words in your words. It was your message to us, was it not? To the followers of Wycliffe? You have translated Latin scripture, the words of Saint Paul, directly, but so cunningly hid it in your text that none but those who know, those who have themselves translated the Bible in secret, would find it.

We know, sister. We who seek to return Christianity to the truth of Christ by means of the scriptures, without intermediary, we who thus need to read of Christ for ourselves, in our own tongue.

I shake my head at him, horrified.

I meant no such thing, I whisper. I say, I did not know the words were exact. I did not, I do not, seek to take scripture away from holy church into my own hands and you may not my voice is raised now, strong,

you may not read it so.

William draws back from me, from the parchment sheaf, from the table, his face suddenly slack with doubt. He glances at Adam, who speaks for the first time:

Peace, mistress, we did not come to distress you. You say you intended no translation and we have no reason to disbelieve you, but you must see how your words have kindled hope in us, that one so blessed as you with your visions would know our cause and long to join us?

Truly, do you not long for the freedom Christ promised and which the church has taken from us?

My voice is firm when I say:

You have not understood. I am not of your thinking and I do not wish to be. Holy church teaches me all. Please leave.

But I cannot meet his gaze.

William slowly and carefully furls the parchment sheaf of my words and replaces it in his tunic, and the two men rise and make for the door. I follow, and watch them walk away, standing sentinel despite the cold. Some twenty yards on, Adam turns and looks at me. I can face him from this distance and I do so, raising my arm in farewell, but I am afraid of what is stirring in my heart.

XXXII

I step back into the cottage and pull the door to, make it fast, banish the cold with a buffer of cloth on the floor against its base, return to my seat at the hearth, watch myself move, notice my hands are not steady. My glance keeps Alice away for now. I need space to reflect.

I have heard of the teachings of John Wycliffe, railing against the corrupt worldly power and wealth of the church, demanding that the priests step aside and allow the ordinary people to receive scripture in their own tongue, in English, so they may learn for themselves the word of God.

I have secretly wondered at the wealth of bishops and the power of priests. When the people lack what they need just to live.

I have wondered why Felicia and I can study so many texts in English but not the source of their wisdom, the Word of God itself, and I have secretly longed to read and copy scripture in English.

I think: Adam saw this in me. And I believe he may return to urge his teaching, and I am afraid.

A mist descends between my seeing and the visions that I saw. I fear they are being taken from me and turned into something they are not and that they are becoming dangerous.

I am not a lawyer to debate a case. I am not a theologian to construct an argument. I cannot defend the visions when I hardly know what they are myself. I know they are truly there when I encounter those who seek counsel, but they are not there in clever words to make sense of the world and God to others. They are living, not dead, and Adam and William can see this and they want the power and the wisdom of the visions for their own cause.

Their own cause which is not without merit.

But oh, Thomas, it was your doing! You tell me so when you next visit. Those words, those exact words, you who con the Latin scriptures as priests must for all our sakes, you formed the words thus, an unintended exact translation: how could I have done so? I know no Latin but what we say at prayer.

I did not blame you then and I do not do so now, even though the followers of Wycliffe have never let me be, even though Bishop Henry remains suspicious of me to this day. When you visited that morning after the visions, and you did not laugh at me, I spoke fast to you of what I had seen, bright and full of the power of the visions, still not recovered, my mind clear in their light but not clever, and you took time to write and make sense of what I had said and if I spoke in words so close to scripture it was you who made them exact, close to Latin scripture as you are.

Hoc enim sentite in vobis quod et in Christo Iesu, Saint Paul wrote to the Philippians. Each soul should feel in him that in Christ Jesu.

The words are true guidance and that is what matters.

I do not blame you because the visit from those we now call Lollards increases the call in me to a secluded life.

From that day the showings turn and turn again in my heart and will not leave my thoughts. They are inciting, dangerous, truthful; the understanding of their meaning is growing and showing itself to me, the words to describe them are multiplying in me. I need to attend to them. They are for everyone, of that I am assured, but I see that they can be taken, they will be taken, in ways over which I have no control and they may become the cause of harm. I do not know if my growing understanding of them is true. To have time and space and peace and above all freedom to examine the greatness that is growing in me! I begin to long for this with a sharpness that is new.

I do not now feel content in my widow's cottage: peace has departed from it; I am known and sought.

I had long been waiting for something, Thomas. A vocation.

And that for which I have been waiting emerges like a pattern on a cloth being woven in me. The thread of the visions is the strongest colour: I know they need my undisturbed solitude for reflection. And there are other threads. The understanding that I could not marry John and live the life of a householder again, however comfortable. The intelligent conversation and reading with the sisters on Elm Hill, the sisters who also showed me that I am not built for hard physical work or arduous charity. The hope that I can give charity nevertheless, by offering the visions' loving wisdom through counsel. The desire to hear the troubled followers of Wycliffe without condoning or condemning. And, taught by my encounter with Isabel, the prayers for the thousands upon thousands of souls who have died in the pestilence without shriving or due ceremony. The children's souls. To pray for the lost children. To receive and transform the grief of this land and all the lands of the world. I know the visions can bring solace to this great grief but I need to learn how.

Not as a householder. Not as a nun. Not as one of the sisters on Elm Hill. I need to be alone and undisturbed, to be Mary, whose listening Jesu himself protected. So what, then? Where is the life to which I am called? I cannot see it.

I speak of these things to you, Thomas, so you know my forming, and you are deeply wise in your listening silence, hardly interjecting a word, listening, listening, so that I can hear too. So is your listening today: drawing my story from me, in more detail than I could have imagined would be possible, memories I did not know were still present in me, drawn from me like a backdraught from an opening door.

You are the open door.

*

In 1377 when the wood anemones have spread their delicate mantle under the budding trees and the sun gently warms the garden again, a letter comes from you, brought by a cathedral servant who is much too interested in Alice. She is blushing as she hands me the folded parchment.

As truly as the spring sun urges life from the dead and buried seed under the earth in our garden, your words urge new life in me. A new life that is to be found in embracing a kind of death.

The Abbess at Carrow is seeking an anchorite for St Julian's Church in Conesford.

1377–1379

XXXIII

A n anchorite.

What is that? I ask you when we meet.

A hermit, living solitary in a cell attached to a church.

I have not heard of such a life, I say. Are there such in Norwich?

There are few in Norwich today, but hermits stand in a long trad-
ition, a line going all the way back to St Anthony of Egypt in the
fourth century. He sought refuge from the busy city by fleeing to
the desert to pray alone, as Jesu did. Since then many have found
different ways to be alone.

To be alone.

My heart moves strangely within me as I repeat your words, with joy
– at least I think it is joy.

Once you have entered the cell, Julian, you never leave it. You die to the world. You are under vows, like a nun, but the vows are made directly to the Bishop and he is responsible for you.

How do I live if I cannot leave the cell? I ask.

You will need friends who will support you, because you cannot work for a living.

John's pension?

And you can have a maid.

Alice! Could I? Would she?

She lives in a room next to your cell so she can come and go for you, to buy and prepare food and serve you. But you are as one who has died to the world, remaining always in your cell attached to the church. You attend mass daily by witnessing it through a window onto the sanctuary. The rest of your prayers you make alone.

Your cell is not entirely enclosed. There is a window onto the world and people come to seek your counsel. Saint Anthony was not left in peace! And nor is an anchorite. Hermits have always been sought after for their wisdom and the holiness they cultivate in their daily prayer and contemplation. So although you are alone in your cell you are also porous to the world and the world can find you. But you can draw a curtain across the window, and your maid should help to protect your solitude.

You stop me from questioning you further.

You will have time to learn more before you make any decision, and before you are accepted in this role. The Abbess will answer many of your questions.

After you have gone I sit by the fireside and reflect with a deep concentration. My heart still moves joyfully within me at your words. I think I should be anxious at the prospect of being bricked up for the rest of my life but I am not. I think I should feel claustrophobic in just imagining such a life but I do not. I love the thought of being left alone to return again and again to the visions that I have barely begun to understand.

I speak to Alice.

Will you be bored? she asks, bluntly.

I smile but think she has a point to her question. Will I? You have told me that I will be sought for my prayers and my counsel but how do you know? What if no one hears of my isolation and those few who do ignore and forget me? Why would anyone visit?

I don't know, I reply.

Alice laughs.

I don't think you will be bored, mistress.

And I am suddenly desperate to know whether she will come with me. I think anything will be bearable if she is there with her strength and her shrewd eyes and her calm common sense. But as before when my mother died, she has a choice. She has family. She did not have to stay with me then and she does not have to come with me now. Then, she chose to live on in the cottage that had been her home since a child. Now, she would be moving to a new place, to a single room next to a hermit, attached to a strange church. Despite my anxiety I know I must not rush her into a decision, but I cannot forbear from saying

I do not know if this is right for me and I do not know if I will be accepted, but will you consider, will you consider *hard*, whether you will be my maid in my seclusion by the church as you are here in this quiet cottage? Because I would love you to come with me.

Yes, she replies. I will consider it.

And that is all she will say for now.

*

I speak to the lay sisters. Their responses are characteristic.

Margaret says

How will you keep healthy if you cannot walk and feel the sun on your face?

Berta says

The widows will miss you. But they can visit you, can't they?

Matilda says

What will you wear?

And Felicia says

> I have heard lately of a manuscript written about a hermit called Richard Rolle. I will find out if we can borrow it.

She succeeds and we spend an evening at the house on Elm Hill studying the script, written by nuns from Hampole in the north, which has only lately been brought to Norwich. Richard Rolle sought a life that met the call in him without knowing or seeing anywhere what that life was to be. He felt a fierce bodily heat of love but it was only kindled in him when he was alone and could concentrate. He created his own hermit's life, making himself a habit out of his sister's dresses, eliciting scorn and abuse, exiling himself in pursuit of silence. His story moves me. He too had to learn how to be true to his own calling.

Felicia understands the choice I am moving towards and is warm in her support for me. But when we speak on our own she says

> Your visions are compelling and there is much to say about them, much there that will help others, but we both know they do not sit comfortably with all that holy church teaches us. I want to be sure you are not choosing this life in order to hide your wisdom away from the world, as women so often do.

No, Felicia, I say. The visions are for others and I must offer them. But I need to reflect on their meaning in safety, in a place where I will not be seen and interrupted. I know they may be dangerous—

And if you stood on a hilltop and told the world openly about them you would be silenced, Felicia cuts across me and her voice holds bitterness. Or your words would be stolen by a man and claimed as his, or believed to have come from a man. Though Thomas has never claimed authorship of your text, some still insist that he must be, for a woman could never have seen or known such things.

So I have to find my own way, I reply. Like Richard Rolle. He had to wear women's clothes, remember!

We both laugh at the irony.

I will find my own way to tell the visions' truth, in my own room, on my own terms, and nobody need know till I am ready to tell it.

Felicia is satisfied.

The others do not understand my decision so well, but they support me nevertheless.

Will you visit me? I ask timidly.

You will not be left in peace, says Berta. Of course we will come.

*

I tell Isabel of my possible calling.

Where is the anchorhold? she asks, when I have tried again to explain what an anchoress is.

St Julian's, at Conesford, I reply.

We must visit your namesake church, she says. I want to see what your grave is like. Don't you?

I cannot resist her, chiefly because I too really wish to see it.

Isabel is known, but I can be incognito. Alice wants to come with us, which fills me with gladness because it means she is thinking seriously about joining me, but we do not want to draw too much attention to ourselves. To her deep annoyance, I tell her she has to stay behind.

But when Isabel arrives on her palfrey and her groom leads one for me, I look at the horse the groom is riding, and I look at Alice who is standing crossly by the door, and I say

Could Alice ride with the groom?

Isabel turns to him and without a word he shifts forward in his saddle and holds out his hand to Alice, who gives a joyful whoop and runs to climb up and sit pillion behind him, her hands tightly fastened around his waist.

Isabel and I are seated astride, like huntswomen. We move forward, followed by the groom and Alice, clip-clopping through the trees. I feel the warm sun on my back, the rippling strong movements of the horse beneath me, and I notice how the things of nature are even more alive to me as I feel their life through the life of the magnificent beast that bears me. The sharp green new leaves of the birches shimmering in the light, the intoxicating smell of the may, its frothy blossom bud-bursting on the blackthorn, the new ferns unfolding, the springy grass under the horses' hoofs, this twisted tree trunk and the ivy that clings to it, the rich fresh green that is emerging everywhere. Seeds germinate, sap rises, birdsong erupts, spirit lifts and expands and loves all that is made: it is so very good.

I am knowing and loving God's green world more deeply than ever, even as I am proposing to withdraw from it.

We emerge from the trees into an open field and Isabel looks at me and laughs a devilish laugh and dares me to ride faster. How can I refuse? I am alarmed when the horse begins to trot, jiggling me so much I fear I will fall, but Isabel calms me, tells me to clasp his body with my thighs so I can really feel the movement of the palfrey and match my body's movement to his, not jiggling on him, and she lets me try this till I'm comfortable, and then, excitement rising in her voice, her horse pawing and snorting and pulling at her restraining hands, my own horse responding, she tells me to sit firm into my saddle, shorten my reins, keep my head up, my heels down and my shoulders back and go! Her horse flies forward and mine follows with a leap into a thundering rush that truly feels like flying and it is so free and terrifying and I clutch the horse with my thighs and keep my head up and I dare not look behind me to see how Alice fares. And then I somehow soften into the speed and it no longer seems too fast, rather that the horse is moving at the speed of the world and we are all flying in exhilarating joyful exuberant nature . . . and then gradually Isabel brings her horse down to a trot, and mine follows, and then to a walk, and we calm ourselves, breathing deeply and gently, and I can feel my horse calming beneath me, and all our heartbeats slow, and quiet descends, and we walk like this across the Bishop Bridge into the city, following the bend of the river to Conesford and the church of St Julian, my future home, perhaps.

From my seat on my powerful flying palfrey, it looks small. Enclosed, and small.

XXXIV

We ride up to the entrance and wait until Alice and the groom have caught up with us. We dismount, and the groom takes the reins from us and leads the horses away.

The church is grey stone, its stubby tower built towards heaven, not with the elegance of a spire but with a stable determined intent, open to heaven rather than pointing at it. The anchorhold is to the side of the church, built against its southern wall, back from the road.

I am adjusting my wimple and ensuring my face is veiled as the priest comes running out. He stumbles on his cassock and we both reach out instinctively to stop him falling. His figure is lean, tall, but bent over with age. His hair is long and white and his clean-shaven face is lined; deep grooves either side of a mouth made by smiling or dissatisfaction or both; he is smiling now at us as he straightens and releases our steadying hands.

Sisters, aah, aah, that is to say, my lady,

he stutters, looking more closely at our dress, reading Isabel's status, welcome. Aah, aah, what brings you here? How may I serve you?

Isabel glances at me and sees I wish to remain as inconspicuous as I can. Alice is nowhere to be seen.

Father, she bows her head a little,

thank you for your welcome and please forgive our coming upon you unexpectedly and unannounced. I am Isabel, Countess of Suffolk, and this is my companion.

My lady, there is no trouble. The church is empty but I am due to say mass shortly.

And we shall stay to hear it, says Isabel decidedly.

But first, I wonder, she glances at him, her voice less imperious, might we see the anchorhold for which your church is known? I have heard that it stands empty and we have never seen the inside of such a cell before.

The priest hesitates.

It is not just idle curiosity, I assure you, she adds. I respect and admire the devotion of the recluse and I want to understand better what their life is like. And,

she pushes her request home to success, entirely unexpected by me,

my family wishes to support a solitary in return for his prayers. It may be that the next incumbent of your cell will be that person. I would so like to learn more.

The priest looks gratified, taken by her pleas and her promises.

My lady, dear sister, please, come.

He leads the way into the church, talking all the while.

I am Walter and have been priest here for many years. A fine church and a faithful community, I am blessed with my work . . .

though his face did not quite reflect the satisfaction he protested

I-I was intended for the Bishop's chaplain once, because I am of good family, I think of some connection with yours, my lady, but another was favoured and I was given this benefice instead.

Isabel moves her head in a gesture of mild irritation.

Where was I? Oh yes.

Walter leads us along the southern aisle.

This is indeed a rare chance to see the inside of a recluse's home before it is occupied again.

We should not enter

he adds hastily as Isabel moves with confidence towards a doorway in the wall just before the rood screen.

We must preserve the sanctity of the cell. But you can look from the portal, now unbricked.

Isabel and I stand side by side at the doorway to the anchorhold observing, our backs to the still-vocal Walter who has returned to his ancestors and faded hopes of preferment. The sound of his voice recedes as I look into the cell.

There are three steps down from the church to the room, which is nearly square, about the size of my solar; it would take a woman of my height ten paces to cross it from north to south, perhaps twelve paces from east to west. The ceiling is high, making the room spacious though cold. It is not damp. Sunlight enters through the window on the south wall, where people will come to seek counsel. Another window on the north wall, to the left of the portal where we stand, opens the anchorhold to the sanctuary, through which the anchorite – I? – may participate in the mass. There is a window in the western wall, its light shadowed by another cell beyond, I see, where the servant will live, to be the anchorite's connection with the world; she will come and go to bring food and take away waste. There are no doors for me save the temporary portal through which Isabel and I look, which will be bricked up when I enter and remain sealed until after I die.

No doors.

The eastern wall has no physical piercing but the crucifix hangs on it, above an altar; it is a window to heaven, the most important opening in the room. There is a table and chair, simply carved, in the south-west corner, and a truckle bed covered with a coarse grey woollen blanket in the south-east corner. There is a fireplace in the western wall. The floor is covered with fresh rushes. The air is cold but sweet. It is very, very quiet.

And my soul reaches forward to it.

Isabel touches my arm and I come awake and realise that she has been attending to the priest's chatter, keeping him occupied, to give me space and time to gaze at what might be my future dwelling.

Father Walter is about to say mass, Isabel says.

The church has other occupants now, gathering for the service, and I nod and put myself in shadow behind Isabel, veiled by my wimple. Thank goodness.

Confiteor Deo omnipotente . . . Father Walter intones, beginning the mass. I confess to You, Almighty God . . .

I find it hard to remain solemn. Walter stumbles over the *Confiteor*, cannot find the Epistle reading and nearly misses the Gospel altogether. He fumbles on the altar for the communion cup and wafer. Mass pennies are not collected. A small boy, the server, calmly and efficiently corrects where he can, finding the page for the Epistle, whispering to remind him about the Gospel, helping to gather the elements for communion by standing on tiptoe at the altar to reach them. He is patient, and from their tolerant waiting I see the people are used to their priest and love him nevertheless, but I also see Isabel's shoulders start to shake and now laughter wells up in me too. We are visitors, we cannot show disrespect, but that only makes our control harder to sustain.

For now Father Walter has stopped reciting the long prayer of consecration of the bread and wine, just at the high moment of the mass
when he has spoken *Hoc est enim corpus meum*, this is my body, and
would lift up the consecrated wafer, Christ incarnate and resurrected,
our Saviour in the flesh, present with us now, and that is what we are
all here to see. But Walter does not move. The boy, kneeling reverently with his head bowed, starts into wakefulness and looks up at
Walter and tugs his arm. As he does so, the wafer that should have
been on the altar before the priest being transformed into the body
of Christ falls from Walter's capacious sleeve. It must have caught
there and Walter, intoning the prayer, had not noticed its absence in
the paten over which his hands had been hovering until he needed to
lift it up for his congregation to see and worship.

We are held, spellbound in this moment of crisis. For if the wafer was
in his sleeve not on the paten as he prayed, is it consecrated? Is it in
fact the body of Christ or still just a piece of unleavened bread? In the
silence of this moment of indecision which expands till it feels like
eternity, I try so hard to hold my laughter and fail in a terrible,
embarrassing snort which bursts from me, muffled only a little by
my veil and the cough I try to turn it into, and it echoes round and
round the silent stone church and my eyes are streaming and so now
is my nose and with relief I see Walter pushed by the boy into raising
the wafer, consecrated or not, and we fall to our knees and worship
Christ anyway.

In principio erat Verbum erat apud Deum . . .
In the beginning was the Word and the Word was with God . . .

Father Walter finally reaches the end of the mass with the words of
John's Gospel.

We kiss our thumbnails at *in principio* and Isabel and I walk shakily out of the church and only allow ourselves the freedom to laugh when we are some distance away, and then we laugh until our sides ache.

I think that Father Walter will provide good entertainment if I become his church's anchoress, but I also write to you, Thomas, to tell you what we have seen and learned and to ask you if you will be my guide and confessor after I enter the anchorhold, if I am to do so.

XXXV

Daughter, your fame goes before you. Bishop Henry has heard of your visions and I myself have read your account of them. He thinks you are audacious to have written and published them, but that your holiness is exemplary. Your protestations of the authority of holy church even more so.

Perhaps, the Bishop wonders, you protest too much?

One noble eyebrow lifts. My interrogator is a priest in the Bishop's household, whose full figure fills the high carved seat, his arms resting on its arms, his forefinger tapping. He looks at me across the letter-strewn table between us.

I am standing in the Abbess's wood-panelled parlour at Carrow, supplicant to the life of an anchoress. The Abbess is present and she outranks this emissary, but she is not the one to conduct the interview and he is in her chair. She sits straight-backed against the wall, her sharp lapis-blue eyes and firm mouth square-framed by her black and white wimple. Her face is disapproving but not of me, I feel, rather of this upstart priest who does not understand the enclosed life.

I look steadily back at him. The interview will decide whether I am to enter the anchorhold of St Julian's in Conesford. I am sure now that this is my calling. The Bishop's man may not see it so.

Holy church has been my source of truth all my life, I say. It tells me what is needful to know of sin and damnation. It shrives me of my sins. It tells me what is true of our Lord who died on the rood for us and who makes place for us in heaven, we who are saved.

Hmm, good, yes.

He clears his throat. I know my answer is exemplary. I have left out all the questions my visions have raised in me. What is holy church, I wonder in my heart, but do not say.

I am the Bishop's agent in this matter, and I must report to him in full. He needs to know that you are capable of sustaining the life of an anchorite spiritually and physically. You will make your vows to the Bishop alone, to him alone you will swear obedience, and he will be responsible for you.

Yes, Father, I reply.

There is a long, unquiet pause. The priest is looking for words.

There are few anchorites in Norwich and they are all men. First three, now two. One could not endure the life he had chosen, and lost his mind.

These are hard words to hear.

It is a demanding calling, and not one the Bishop favours, continues the priest. He does not think it natural for lay people to enclose themselves singly like this. He would not have sought another had not the Lady Abbess – he looks at her and bows slightly – asked for one.

And he is not at all certain that a woman has the necessary strength.

There is a loud rustle as the Abbess shifts in her seat. Her voice is crisp:

The Bishop—

But the priest raises his hand for silence and says

Daughter, you should know that the anchorite who lost his mind was the occupant of the cell you now seek to enter.

The Abbess, who was ready to argue, is silenced. I am shocked. Father Walter did not mention it, but he was absent-minded and too distracted by Isabel's high status. It is more strange that the Abbess said nothing to me during our interview before this one, when she was assuring herself of my vocation.

The Bishop's man is speaking again, his voice kindly, tempting me:

You could live easily and well as a widow in your home, and move about the world as you wish, attend mass daily for your soul. Or you could enter a convent if you seek a life of prayer. You have no need to brick yourself up alive in a tomb.

In the waiting silence I picture the cell Isabel took me to see, and I enter it with my mind's eye. In my mind, in my heart, seated there in the cell, I do not feel the presence of an unhappy spirit and I do not feel I am in a tomb.

I am in a room of my own.

I will pray for the man.

So we must be very certain that you have a vocation to this life, the Bishop's man is saying, watching me.

What calls you to be a recluse?

I make myself pause before replying. I do not say: I must have the freedom of mind and heart that only solitude brings, freedom and time to revisit the visions and say to myself first what they mean before showing them to others. Time to keep revisiting because there are so many layers of meaning to penetrate, meanings that may be dangerous to speak aloud. I do not say: indeed I crave to be left alone. I crave silence and withdrawal. I do not say: by anchoring myself so closely to holy church she cannot hold me apart from herself and inspect and interrogate my unorthodox seeing.

I do say:

I am called to live my life in contemplation of all that God has shown me, undistracted by the world. I am called by the strength of my love for my Lord, who showed Himself to me so fully. I am

called to ponder my visions of his dying and test their truth against
the teaching of holy church,

well, that is nearly true, and the Bishop's man is nodding, listening,
not dismissing my words,

and I want nothing more than to attend to this. I cannot hope for
a better place than as a recluse in order to do so.

I pause again. I do not say: I see the waves of grief and loss that pass
through the land, sent underground by the longing to move on and
forget, but rumbling there still, and I am filled with the call to pray
not just for the souls of those who ask, but of all those unknown to
me who died in the pestilence, the thousands upon thousands who
fell unshriven and without ceremony into their graves. All the dead
children. I do not say: yes, the pestilence evokes penitence in our
hearts but the penitence is not, should not be, that of blame and
guilt. It should be soft, softly knowing we all fail, and in our acceptance that we cannot prevent loss or push away suffering, our hearts
can melt not harden and the love that has the power to dissolve the
bitterness that is in the grief can flow like a great wave itself, greater
than any wave of sickness, and be admitted. I do not say: I will pray
so openly and fully and porously and transparently that the penitence will become active love to transform the grief back into what
seeded it, for the grief in our hearts is born of love. And the aching
souls of those who have survived their children can be soothed in the
balm of that love.

These are audacious thoughts, more audacious than the priest already
thinks me.

I do say:

> I am called to intercede for the souls of the many dead from the pestilence.

The Bishop's man nods again.

> Yes, good.

I do not say: I have seen that I can help those who seek, by listening and watching as the love that magnified in the visions magnifies in them. What happens is of the Holy Ghost, the spirit stirs, but it feels like magic because I do not know where the words I may speak then come from, and if there are no words of mine because the speaker has said all that is needed for the love to heal, it feels even more magical. I need to sit alone to offer this concentrated listening, and I need to be alone afterwards to recover, for it drains me. I think: if I say these things I will sound like a witch.

I do say:

> I am called to hear the troubles of my fellow Christians and to respond with counsel, not as a learned woman, for I am anything but that, but with simple words from Jesu as I have been taught by holy church.

Another nod. Good. I have spoken of three callings to the three practices of the anchorite, of contemplative prayer, prayer of intercession, and counsel. I have spoken with clarity and steadiness and modesty, and the priest's face is softer, and his voice is less imperious.

Julian.

He says my name for the first time.

The Abbess tells me you wish to keep the name Julian because it is also the name of the church's saint where your anchorhold would be. Saint Julian. Him, not you!

He permits himself a smile.

No, Father. But I am glad to share his name.

And the Bishop is content that you should. Now, to your physical means.

The tension in the room eases as he turns to the letters on his desk.

This letter from the Countess of Suffolk, Lady Isabel, who wishes your prayers for her family, commends you highly. She says you have restored her trust in Christ Jesu and nurtured her faith and she is strong because of you. She is known for her holiness and her care for the poor in Suffolk.

The lady Isabel is a holy woman, I say.

I picture us flying across fields on her palfreys, her laughter, her freedom. Yes, she is holy.

And she will support you financially, of course. As will . . .

he shuffles the sheets of parchment,

> John Plumpton, who says you gave him the merchant house and
> his livelihood, and he has undertaken to provide for you for as
> long as you live.

> You will have sufficient resources for yourself and your maid. That
> is well, daughter. The Bishop needs this reassurance.

Isabel has told me she will support me, but I did not expect this
from John. Our last conversation was filled by his strong urging
that I should work, contribute to the business; he can find suit-
able employment for me, he says, and his children love their
adopted aunt. I should return to the city and rejoin the world,
not shrink from it. Not like this. Not in a living tomb. He gave
me little space and no encouragement to state my own wishes,
and I thought in his disapproval he could withdraw my pension
even though I had a right to it. But he must have listened to what
I was able to say, or watched my face more carefully than I realised, while he spoke.

> I am grateful for their help and they are assured of my prayers.

I mean it with all my heart.

> And you have a maid willing to come with you and serve
> you?

This remains the greatest blessing and the strongest note of steadfast-
ness in me as I face the prospect of entering the anchorhold for the

rest of my life. For Alice has agreed to come. She told me that while Isabel and I were inside the church looking at the anchorhold and attending mass, she was exploring the outside. She said she could see into the room that would be hers and she thought it comfortable enough, well built, dry. It stands against the church to the west of the anchorhold, a separate building with its own entrance to the street, but with a little door opening in its east wall facing the window opening to my cell. One step outside between the two, she said. And she said there is a patch of ground on the other side of my cell that had once been a garden, where she could grow good food for us to eat. And finally she said

Yes, I will come and serve you. You still need me. I am cunning; you are not. I am worldly; you are not and will become less so over time, hidden away in your cell.

She is adamant. And I am so very relieved.

Yes, my maid Alice will come, and willingly.

Then I think that is all. But I would ask you, daughter,

and now the priest's face is very gentle, fatherly, and I am disconcerted,

How prepared – truly, daughter – how prepared are you for the life of a hermit?

He waits for my answer. No longer the Bishop's man, now a fellow human asking in kindness, in genuine concern.

I cannot know if I will feel constrained by the walls of my cell, I say,

and stop. I cannot know. Or rather, of course I will feel constrained. Oh, I will miss the living things of God's creation and the freedom to walk among them! What can I say to prove to him or to me that I will be all right? I can imagine what the life will be but until I live it I do not know for certain. I do not know how or even who I will be as I live it.

I have lived alone with my maid for some years now, I say, trying to cover the hesitation in my voice. I am content in my own company and diligent in solitary prayer.

And then I say,

That is all I know.

I cannot pretend a confidence I do not feel.

Hmm.

There is another long silence. The Bishop's man fastens his eyes on me, one hand softly stroking his chin. I return his gaze, trying to look not boldly but modestly, but still, I do not drop my eyes. I must allow myself to be examined. He is no upstart, he has done this before, and knows of those who survive, and those who do not, this life towards which I am moving.

Then he shifts in his seat, and gathers the letters into a pile. He turns to the Abbess, and I see her nod. Once. Firmly.

I will recommend your admittance as an anchoress in the church of St Julian, Conesford, he says.

And abruptly rises and departs without looking back, leaving me staring at the space where his eyes had been, my mind entirely blank.

XXXVI

As a seed must die in order to live. So will you be.

Seated in her parlour in her own chair, the Abbess leans towards me as she speaks. Her piercing lapis-blue eyes and thin lips and angular frame and sharp mind are focused upon her task: to prepare me for the life that has chosen me, that I have chosen. I think, from the words of the Bishop's agent and the care she is taking now, that much is hanging on this. The last incumbent of the anchorhold of which her convent is sponsor did not survive. The Abbess is replacing him, and with a woman, the first woman recluse in Norwich, and the Bishop favours neither proposition. She – and I – must prove him wrong. There is precedent: there have been many anchoresses before, not in Norwich but in the North, for whom *The Guide for Anchoresses* has been written, and she has a copy, and she is determined. She sees me nearly every day, instructing, questioning, conversing and encouraging me to speak openly in response. I take her instruction and advice seriously, though much of it I do not fully understand or value until I am in the anchorhold and then her wisdom carries me through some of the worst times.

I stay at the convent in Carrow for my time of preparation, wearing not the dress of a postulant but the simple linen gown and cap of an anchoress suggested by the *Guide*: a novice anchoress. My new clothes fit me well, I feel light and free in them, free from the wimple's constraints, free from the burden of status that clothes always confer.

I learn the nuns' discipline, singing the Hours with them as I will when solitary. I had wondered about the cramping lack of movement enforced by enclosure but the rigours of the office as we stand, kneel, beat our breasts, sit, bow a little, bow low, bow to the ground and prostrate ourselves fully, ensure our bodies are as engaged as our minds and hearts in the prayers we speak and sing. The *Guide* states that I may if I wish embody my prayer even more than the nuns do, by practices such as raising my arms to heaven and bowing from the waist while still abed, at the moment of my waking.

The Hours of our prayers beat the timing of Christ's passion. We rise at midnight to sing Matins when he was praying and weeping blood in the Garden of Gethsemane. These are the hours of the night when the human heart can give way to despair and our prayer is quiet light holding steady in the darkness. Then we return to rest until Lauds and Prime at six o'clock, when Christ was tried by the temple priests. The dawn is promised and our prayer welcomes the day:

Jubilemus Deo, Salutari nostro . . .
Let us make a joyful noise unto the God of our salvation . . .

At nine o'clock when Christ was tried by Pilate and flogged, we say Terce:

Sana me, Domine, et sanabor: salvum me fac, et salvus ero: quoniam laus mea tu es . . .

Heal me, O Lord, and I shall be healed: save me, and I shall be saved, for thou art my praise . . .

Then we study, reading the Psalms or stories of the saints or other texts. The convent library is well stocked. During these morning hours I meet the Abbess for instruction but when I am not with her I con my breviary, for when I say the Hours as a solitary I do not want to stumble over the Latin. I want to understand it.

One wintry morning after Terce I am called to the guest parlour to meet visitors and find, to my great delight, Felicia and Margaret waiting there for me. Felicia's face is radiant with her rare smile as she speaks:

We have gifts for you, furnishings for your anchorhold.

And Margaret, with the reverence of one conveying holy relics, lays three books in my arms, books I recognise, bound in thick, precious vellum. I cry out with joy as I examine each one. Dionysius's *Hid Divinity*, *The Cloud of Unknowing* and *The Mind's Road to God* by Bonaventure. The sisters' own copies.

We are copying them again for ourselves, says Felicia, rightly interpreting my anxious look. You do not leave us bereft. And you need these books now.

Precious, precious gifts, written in the sisters' own hands, mostly Felicia's but also Matilda's. Parchment prepared by Margaret and Berta, sewn and bound by Matilda, handled and lovingly read by them all. I had only the scraps of parchment of my own copying at Felicia's encouragement. Just a few lines. And now I have whole volumes.

I have no appointment with the Abbess today and I study *The Cloud of Unknowing* for the rest of the morning.

At noon, when Christ hangs in shame on the rood, a priest comes to say mass. At the moment when Christ dies the priest lifts the consecrated bread, now the body of Jesu, and we contemplate and sometimes receive the risen Lord.

Before our midday meal we sing Sext, when darkness falls on the world after Christ has died:

Nemine quidquam debeatis, nisi ut invicem diligatis . . .
Owe no man anything but to love one another . . .

We eat the peasant food I will eat in my anchorhold: rye bread and pottage made of oats, green peas, leeks, onion, garlic, herbs, white beans. No meat. Sometimes fish. A little beer. No milk on fast days. And then we rest.

Nones is at three after noon:

In timore incolatus vestri tempore conversamini . . .
Converse in fear during the time of your sojourning here . . .

Then work, some in the garden, some cleaning the chapel, some copying texts in the scriptorium. Sometimes I work with the nuns but mostly the time is given to me to practise the contemplative prayer required of the anchoress. I am Mary, not Martha, the Abbess reminds me. It is for others to care for the material world while I must discover God within.

It is not easy, because there is no structure. I am simply to wait upon God. The Abbess encourages patience and gives me some tools: as *The Cloud of Unknowing* teaches, I can have a little word to say, a word such as Jesu, or love, repeated without adding any further prayer, repeated so as to turn my attention again and again to God, inward not outward, a word that falls silent once it has led me to God's presence. Or I can hold one simple image in my mind's eye in the same way: not an object of worship but a guide that takes my hand and leads me to deep inwardness.

> Do not dwell on your visions now, the Abbess counsels, unless it is shown to you that you must. Use the time you have with us to prepare for your deeper understanding of them. Learn to go with your mind to your heart, and wait.

I turn to this prayer with joy, it feeds a deep hunger within me, but it takes patience and trust: trust that God will simply be without any action on my part. Why should He be present to me without any means? But the visions have taught me to trust, and I learn some patience with myself.

Vespers is at six after noon when Christ's beloved body was brought down from the cross and placed in the tomb, and we sing the great hymn of Mary:

> *Magnificat anima mea Dominum . . .*
> My soul doth magnify the Lord . . .

It is winter so we eat again. From Easter until Whitsun in high summer there is only one meal in the middle of the day, and the same will be true for me when I am solitary.

We sing Compline at nine after noon, preparing ourselves for sleep, for death, for vigilance through the dark night:

Noctem quietam et finem perfectum concedat nobis Dominus omnipotens. Amen.
May almighty God grant us a quiet night and a perfect end. Amen.

Nunc dimittis servum tuum Domine . . .
Now lettest Thou Thy servant depart in peace, O Lord . . .

In manus tuas Domine, commendo spiritum meum . . .
Into Thy hands, O Lord, I commend my spirit . . .

And then bed.

I cherish these months of preparation. More scaffolded by formal prayer than the life of the lay sisters on Elm Hill, but with the same gentle intent, I find it easy to mimic and, over time, learn the nuns' perseverant constancy in their prayer which regulates each day, seeping into the hours between the Hours, and I grow quiet in their company. The Abbess's wisdom shared with such clarity and care strengthens my spirit. My growing fluency in Latin comforts me and I begin to trust that I will be able to sustain the prayer when I am solitary. I spend as much time as I can outside. We laugh. A lot. I love to be with the nuns.

But the loveliest time of all is spent in contemplative prayer, as I feel the move within me, the turning deep and slow within me, turning and moving inwards, always inwards, and always alone.

May 1379

XXXVII

On a bright spring day the congregation gathers in the church of St Julian, filling the nave, rustling on the benches and murmuring to each other. Many have come to my burial out of curiosity, but those who know and love me are present too. Isabel sits with her husband William, Earl of Suffolk, in the most important seats at the front. Felicia, Berta, Margaret and Matilda are all here, and so are John and Alba and their growing family – there are three children now: Edward and a younger sister, Clemency, hushed by John's side, the babe Arthur cradled in Alba's arms.

You are there, beloved Thomas, as an assistant priest, steady then as you are now, serious, quietly joyful, confident in me taking this drastic action, confident in the truth of the visions that have brought me here, you who did not laugh when I said I raved. Because of that I am here.

*

My face is all that is not covered by the white shift that enwraps me like a shroud, signalling my death. Today is my burial; today is my rebirth.

I stand before the Bishop to make my vows. It is the first time I have seen Bishop Henry and I am surprised by how young he is: my own age perhaps, slender, wiry, hardly taller than I. His figure and presence are made weighty by his mitre, his staff and his cope, which is black to signify his task today, but he is springy, alert, as though ready at any time to enter a fray. He fills the church with his forceful energy, and before him I am so slight, unvested of any status, so solitary, I am already almost not here, and yet his brown eyes fix on mine as though I were a potential assailant with an army.

I vow obedience, chastity, and stability of place.

I will be obedient to my calling and to you, my Bishop.

I will remain in this place till the death of my body.

I will pray.

I will pray.

The Bishop moves to his seat.

And as a dying or dead body would be, I am sprinkled with holy water, and censed, and anointed by a priest, not Father Walter who is mercifully kept to one side, but one of the Bishop's household. He intones:

Per istam sanctam unctionem et suam piisimam misericordiam, indulgeat tibi Dominus quidquid per visium . . .
Through this holy unction and His own most tender mercy may the Lord pardon thee whatever sins thou has committed by sight . . .

And he touches my closed eyelids with holy oil.

And he intones the same words each time as he anoints my ears: *auditorum*, nose: *odoratum*, tongue: *gustum et locutionem*, hands: *tactum*, feet: *gressum*.

I place myself on the ground, prostrate before the altar in the sanctuary, where the coffin would be placed. I am dead now, dead to the world. I lie completely still, and the memory returns of my childhood wish to come close to death, my vain attempt to fulfil my wish then, its fulfilment in the visions, and its fulfilment now.

Only this time, to the world, I am not close to death, I *am* dead.

Dead.

The requiem mass begins.

> *Requiem aeternam dona eius Domine et lux perpetua luceat eius . . .*
> Rest eternal grant unto her, O Lord, and let light perpetual shine upon her . . .

> *Agnus Dei qui tollis peccata mundi*
> Lamb of God, who takes away the sins of the world

> *Dona nobis pacem*
> Grant us peace.

The Gospel reading is the story of Mary and Martha in Luke's Gospel, read in Latin, but I know the story so well now.

Now it came to pass, as they went, that he entered into a certain village: and a certain woman named Martha received him into her house. And she had a sister called Mary, which also sat at Jesus' feet, and heard his word. But Martha was cumbered about much serving, and came to him, and said, Lord, dost thou not care that my sister hath left me to serve alone? Bid her therefore that she help me. And Jesus answered and said unto her, Martha, Martha, thou art careful and troubled about many things:

But one thing is needful: and Mary hath chosen that good part, which shall not be taken away from her.

When the mass ends, with almost no volition at all of my own, I am taken from my place before the high altar through the rood screen to the doorway in the south wall of the church, portal to my anchorhold, my place of prayer and retreat, of loneliness and submission, my last resting place before death, my first grave. The priests who convey me stop at the doorway and release my hands, and at this point I am alone, and alone, by my own deliberate choice, I step down into the room.

The great *dies irae* begins, chanted in relentless, magnificent tones, like a beating drum, and the bell tolls its single, steady note, announcing my death to the world.

Dies irae, dies illa
Solvet saeclum in favilla . . .
Mors stupebit et natura . . .

The day of wrath, that day
Will reduce the world to ashes . . .
Death and nature will marvel . . .

I am in the anchorhold now. The chanting continues, the bell tolls, I turn and kneel at the window into the sanctuary through which I can see the altar and Bishop Henry and the priests, but not the people. Never more the people at prayer.

I am kneeling, my body completely still and steady, and then . . .

Panic rises from my belly to my forehead.

But it is too late to run.

The little doorway is bricked up, one brick upon another, not yet sealed with mortar, that will come later, but sealing me in nevertheless, and my breath is shallow now, my heart beating fast as brick upon brick is placed.

Rex tremendae maiestatis,
Qui salvandos salvas gratis,
Salva me, fons pietatis . . .

King of fearsome majesty,
Who gladly saves those fit to be saved,
Save me, O fount of mercy . . .

The last bricks are laid. The space where the door was is gone. I am buried.

The cantor completes the terrible chant:

Pie Iesu Domine,
Dona eis requiem. Amen.

Merciful Lord Jesus,
Grant me rest. Amen.

XXXVIII

S tillness.

There is a quiet rustling of clothes and patter of feet as the people leave the church, then the thin cry of a baby, Arthur perhaps, rises, piercing the silence: is it a cry of pain or for new life or both? The cry leaves the church with the people and silence returns.

I rise and release the curtain over the squint and I turn to face my cell, my coffin, my small home.

*

I have never felt so fully alive.

*

I am not expecting this. I was expecting to feel tortured by confinement at this moment, as the portal is bricked up, the impervious walls pressing upon me like the walls of my home with Martin in the city, my breath short and shallow, and panic only just kept under control. But the panic I felt when I first kneeled has gone.

At last, at last I am alone, I am at home. My breath is deep and satisfying, like drinking delicious clean water and slaking a thirst I hardly knew I had. I stand in the vast space that feels like the cathedral, made bigger not smaller by the walls, and it is all my own. Grateful relief floods through me like a balm. At last, I can ask the world to recede, and it will. All I have to do is to close the curtain and I will be left in peace. *Dona nobis pacem.* So much space, just for me. And warm! A fire has been lit in the little fireplace, life in new death. I reach with careful fingertips and touch the east wall where my altar stands beneath my crucifix, towards the dawn, towards new life, towards God. There is nothing now between me and God. No thing. I kneel, and weep tears of joy and speak words of thanks, for the time that is granted me here, now. Time, and space, and strength, for the long, slow interior journey, deep into God, God deep into me. I have come home, Thomas! And here, twenty-five years later, I still, gratefully, am.

1379–1380

XXXIX

I learn how to counsel my fellow Christians, for now I am an anchoress I am believed to be able to offer advice.

Each afternoon, after Nones and sometimes before as well, I draw aside my curtain to the world and find a soul waiting to speak, from Norwich, sometimes from further afield. Many become familiar to me. They tell me their news and they seek counsel and I have learned how much to say, which is very little, and how much to remain silent, which is mostly needed. I am not wise and I do not solve their troubles. But I learn to listen with my face turned towards the person speaking, with my heart open to them and my smile warm in encouragement. I never repeat their words to others and they grow in trust, and in their vulnerable speech comes the clarity that reveals what is needful. I ask that they speak from their open heart and do not waste words of hiding, unless they need to start to speak and let the words run for a while until truth becomes evident, as much to them as to me.

And as the words spill from the lips of my visitors, and I receive them, so love arises between us and it cannot be denied. Of that I speak, as the visions have shown me. God is love not wrath. Love not wrath. Does not cease to love however ashamed you feel. Accept the pain of failure and let it grow contrition in you so that you become soft and open to God, so soft that you can turn your sore unyielding neck and see that God has not ceased to regard you with love.

Sometimes I turn to my window and find Isabel's smiling face there. She comes for counsel but she also tells me of her horses and her life and she gives me energy, and after she has gone Alice shows me the good things to eat she has left behind, milk puddings and cheese and roasted meat and fine fruit grown in her orchards and greenhouses. We can only eat such rich food on feast days so at other times we give it away before it spoils.

The sisters visit too, as they promised they would, Felicia most often, and we resume our conversations with a new zest for enquiry.

Scholars come to quarrel and question, often because they have read your text, Thomas, but also because I am a strange being, a woman who is living her own life of prayer. I am at first made anxious by their manner and my own lack of knowledge, but after a time I learn to set aside my qualms, to listen carefully to their words not as a disputatious scholar would, picking holes in their arguments as they seek to pick holes in my story of the visions and my secluded way of life, but by asking questions myself. With some, truly enjoyable conversations emerge as exploration based upon experience, not theory, replaces dispute. With some, what begins as argument ends in counselling. With some, I am given no quarter but berated for being so forward and foolish, a woman, presuming to live alone, calling herself holy, offering counsel. How dare I think for myself!

Alice learns to recognise these unkind scholars and keeps them from my window if she can but she does not always succeed.

Anselm, a friar from the Augustinian house by my cell, visits. Our conversation does not begin well.

Sister Julian, your fame goes before you, he says, not friendly. My brothers and I are curious to know why you came here and how you fare.

Well, thank you, I respond, watching his prying eyes try to look into my cell, and moving to block the window space with my own body.

You know, Anselm says, suppressing what looks to me like a smirk, your predecessor went mad? We are concerned it is the cell that did it, and we cannot believe a woman would be able to withstand pressures that he could not.

I remain silent, inwardly furious. I will not give this man the satisfaction of seeking to justify myself to him. My right to occupy this cell and to live this life has been established by the Abbess and the Bishop and it is none of Anselm's business. But to my surprise his face softens at my failure to argue with him.

Forgive my temerity, sister, he says. We know the former anchorite. His name is Giles; we cared for him in our friary for a short time before he was taken to a hospice where he still lives. I do not mean to be rude. We are concerned, that is all.

I will pray for him, I say, and step back from my window, letting the curtain fall.

Oh, the relief at being able to do this. Anselm has no choice but to leave. But he returns and manages to win over Alice sufficiently so that he can speak with me again, and this time he comes with humility to ask what the visions meant to me, and to tell me of visions he has had that he cannot quite trust. I discover a new skill: I can discern the validity of visions as they are described to me, not because of special knowledge, but by the same careful listening I bring to all my encounters. More visitors come to seek counsel because of this. My fear of being ignored and forgotten could not have been more unfounded, and Alice has to develop a system, making visitors come to her first to be allotted time with the first woman in Norwich to become an anchoress.

The Abbess offers to build a parlour against my window to the world to protect those who come to see me, but this would rob me of the sight of the apple tree Alice has planted in the corner of her garden, of more distant trees and of the night sky, and I ask her only to create a porch roof to keep the rain off those who sit and speak to me. I must be able to touch nature, if only with my eyes. And when the sun comes out and no one is by, I can turn my face to it and feel it warming me, doing me good.

The sun and the sky and the trees do not take my mind from God. They lead me to God.

XL

I learn afresh how to read, more slowly because I have time, silently because there is only myself to hear.

I have my breviary with the words of the Offices, the Psalms and other scripture readings and I continue to stumble over its Latin and learn its meaning by listening, improving all the time. I have time. Slowly, slowly I read Dionysius, Bonaventure, *The Cloud of Unknowing*. Anselm, newly enthusiastic to support my vocation, brings me other books from the library at Austin Friars. I study these and speak of their meaning with him and with Felicia.

I listen to the visiting preachers Father Walter invites. Not all, but some are truly learned and holy and I feel myself nourished in my intellect and my soul by their teaching.

*

I learn again to pray, for I have time now to pray.

The Hours are my anchor in the anchorhold and ground me again and again in my calling. I keep them faithfully, my nights and days measured by them, by the summoning bells of the cathedral which reach my ears, joining my sisters at Carrow and everywhere in Christendom, speaking and chanting the words of the Offices to hold my fellow humans, to heal the world.

Sometimes the words are enough. I learn them, recite them and listen to them. They come slowly with my listening, and then the Office takes longer, fills my day.

Sometimes the words I am given slip quickly from me and my deeper prayer with words is in my reading.

And I learn how to pray for those who have asked for my prayers, and for those who could not. Each day I learn. Each day I am shown. I kneel, and bring those for whom I am to pray into my heart. I allow my thoughts to quieten, I gently lay aside my notions of how to do this and my fears of not knowing how to do this, and I speak out loud the name of the first person. Alba. I present that name and that person to Jesu on the cross before me, to the God He is. I do not ask for anything because I do not know what is needed. I only present the name, Alba, and keep my attention gently focused on that name and that person and openness to God so that after a while I feel nothing of myself, and I feel no apartness between Alba and God. God is frayed and Alba is frayed and the loose threads begin to weave together to make a new cloth. Or God and Alba are melting together. Or sometimes it seems that Jesu holds out his arms and takes Alba into them and embraces her so fully that every part of her is warmed and loved and reassured. And then to the next name, William. William. And I disappear and God's embrace returns to take this soul who has sought my prayers into His arms and comfort him.

Each day I pray for Giles whose troubles do not haunt this cell.

And I pray for the souls who died unshriven in the pestilence, who could not ask for my prayers, for my daughter and my husband, and for all the others unknown to me. This is harder. I have no names to speak only thousands upon thousands of souls who flood through me as though passing through my body; they feel like water but it is water that passes through me, and I try to remain open and steady and let it happen, and it asks me to become enormous so all the souls can pass through, and the grief that is the water that passes through is enormous and intense and if I am not steady can hurt like the pain of hell itself. The grief rises and falls and by the end of my time of prayer it has abated, like a great fit of sobbing that eventually cries itself out, and I am empty as if it were I who weep. I do not know what this means. But I am given this task each day and I trust it.

And I give time each day to simple contemplation, each morning after I have spent time reading, before Sext, and in the evening after Vespers. When every thought, every means to prayer, is set aside, and I follow the Abbess's guidance, using no words save perhaps one word, and with that little word gently repeating, my soul quietens and softens and the little word enters me and brings me to deep, deep rest in my soul, which becomes no place. Everything has dissolved, even the little word, and there is only God beholding in me and I am no one and no where.

It is not always like this. But I keep faith with the time I give to contemplation even if all I meet is aridity.

Often in that space which is no place, in that deep silence of no thing, my visions return. They come in a single moment, like a great company of musicians playing sweet music together, each with their different parts. In quiet awe I watch steadily, making an effort not to go towards one sound or another, but staying quite still inside myself. Then a single melody, one of the visions, moves out of its place in the polyphony and presents itself to me.

I thank thee for thy travails.

And once more I learn and feel with all I am that the striving of that tender little girl to appease an angry God, and the young mother who thought she had killed her family by her negligence and confessed her guilt again and again, and the recluse whose prayer is sometimes as dry as a land that never saw water, that those people I have been and I am are always loved; that their striving is gratefully received and there need be no anxiety in the striving; that the failures are what make me, forge me, teach me, that if God loves me so much in my failures and my trying then I must love that child, that young woman, that weakling of a hermit that I am. Jesu thanks me, not for my success, but for my failure and my trying.

And I feel another layer peel away as my seeing sharpens and my understanding grows and my feeling of who I am and who God is deepens.

I learn that I will always carry the wounds of the vulnerable striving little girl and the guilty young mother and the unevenly praying hermit. This prayer does not cure me of the pain of failure. It teaches me, again and again, to receive the pain, as Jesu did, as God does, and let it transform me.

I learn that this deepening and this peeling and this self-forgiveness will never stop. There is no end to the depth of God. I do not become and will never become wise. I will learn and keep on learning. And so acceptance and gratitude grow in me, and as I speak to you now, Thomas, I can see how my soul is settled, not in a task finished but in a task never completed, mostly a joyful task, and the visions are my means.

In those early years the visions return to me, not with the shock and power of their first appearance, but gently and with softly growing clarity, like a mist slowly dissolving in sunshine that warms and a sun that glows more richly as I contemplate. I wait patiently, with no urgency. I have been granted all the time there is. I do not try to make anything of what I see. I hold no expectation or assumption that I know anything at all.

The visions teach me patience. And to be silent about them for now, for even as my fame grows and my counsel is sought, there are those who do not cease to regard me with suspicion, and the visions, were they to be more fully expressed, would only confirm their worst fears. For not only am I a woman entering worlds that only men should occupy, I am also dallying with heresy, some say, in the text of my visions that has been published, dallying with the teaching of Wycliffe, with the likes of William and Adam, and that will lead to no good, some say.

XLI

The fire has died and my feet are cold.

I cannot sleep. I rise from my bed and push aside the heavy curtain of my window to the world, whose turning has brought it to the darkest time. All things, even the plants and the planets, are sleeping, but I cannot.

It is the darkest time when anxiety rises and the mind is too tired to make sense of its fears and allay them.

What have I done?

I kneel before my altar, and try to turn my thoughts to God. They will not turn. All I can think is: what have I done?

I stand up suddenly. I cannot abide my silent prison. I pace: ten paces to the south till I bump into the external wall, twelve paces from east to west, bumping again into the walls of my prison. Alice stirs and calls to see if I need anything but I make my voice calm and tell her to go back to sleep.

I feel like a wild animal caged. For ever.

What have I done?

I have put myself in prison and now I do not know why. God is absent from me, I have no feeling of His presence, I do not know where He is. I glance wildly in the direction of the crucifix on the wall but it is too dark and I cannot see Jesu and I cannot feel Him. There is no God here and the life I have chosen is meaningless. I am a fool, a miserable disbelieving fool, who has banished from herself a world that might have comforted her, distracted her at least.

And I suddenly feel upon my shoulder the grip of John's hand, as real as though he were here. It torments me. I long for him to be here. My body is on fire and I long for him.

He is not here, there is *nothing* here to stop this terrible growing empty hole inside me, a sucking dark blackness that is taking me over and will soon draw all that I am into its depths and I will melt into utter, unhappy, lost despair. No joy. No love. No lightness. I am alone. Dark and lost and alone.

Was Giles my predecessor so tortured? It is unendurable.

I resume my pacing, pacing, a wild animal caged, on fire and alone.

What have I done?

My pacing speeds up, growing in madness as I walk towards the wall by Alice's cell and *push* at it with my hands, away and round and back to the east wall and *push* it with my hands, then across to the external wall and *push* it with my hands, and back to the church wall and *push* it with my hands. Nothing moves. I am here and I cannot leave and now claustrophobia is growing in me and I am going to scream I am going to scream and that will bring a terror to me from which I will never return and nor will Alice.

I stand still.

What am I doing?

I force myself to lie back down on my bed, to stop myself feeling the walls of my prison, to make it bigger by making myself smaller. Panic beating in me still, shallow gulping breaths of air, there is not enough air, and now, only now, does the Abbess's advice come to me. Breathe deeply, she said. When the walls of your cell press upon you, breathe deeply, and prayer will return.

And at the next gulping gasping breath my body snatches from the stifling air, I stop. And hold it. Just for a moment, for a pause, and even though I do not feel as though I have much breath in me, I let it out, and I let it out slowly from a slack, open jaw, haaaah, all the way out, and wait a moment before drawing breath again. I have a tiny amount of control now. An opening to the possibility of calm. This next breath I take, I fill my lungs like a fish with gills, and when they seem full, I deliberately and carefully take a small sip more of air. I wait, and then I release the breath slowly, haaaah, and when it seems all gone I deliberately, carefully, let a little more out, and wait, and draw breath in again, receiving the air gently, the air all around me which does not run out. And now my breath is slowing and my heart is quietening. I do not let myself think *what have I done?* but obedient to the wisdom of the Abbess I take my necklace of prayer beads and feel each one hard in my fingers as I pray *Ave Maria, gratia plena, Dominus tecum*, Hail Mary, full of grace, the Lord is with thee. One bead for each repetition of the prayer, feeling the bead in my fingers as though the prayer were being spoken there, in the touch of my fingers and the beads and in my breath. And the touch of the beads is real, the beads are here, banishing the feeling of John's grasp on my shoulder, John who is not here. I am breathing Our Lady, repeating the prayer, over and over, not making sense of the words as I murmur them, making a meditation of them, letting *Maria*, mother, breathe into me her truth without any interference from my restless unhappy mind, just saying the words over and over, slowly, letting my breath quieten and deepen with the words, placing myself entirely in the arms of my absent God through the words and in the touch of the beads and in my breathing, helpless and lost and frightened as I am, lying on my little bed in my little cell, alone in the enormous dark night, over and over again repeating *Ave Maria, gratia plena, Dominus tecum. Ave Maria. Ave Maria.* Mother.

The distant cathedral bell tolls calling me to Matins. This simple prayer is my Matins tonight and I do not cease my meditation. And somewhere in the midst of the ever-quietening cycle of my lost child's prayer, I fall asleep.

*

I describe one night to you, Thomas, but as you know I have many, many such nights. I still do, and though the wild animal is tamed, sometimes she rises again and paces with anger. Nights when God goes from me, when I do not know what I am doing in this cell, when I feel useless, alone and afraid. Sometimes I can turn quickly to the beads to quieten my mind and comfort my soul, sometimes I have to pace or sit or kneel in dumb anguish for hours before I can meditate again. It is like an illness that falls upon my mind, and yet, though I am drained the next day, I am also cleansed and purged, and I have come to understand these nights are behovely. I have come to understand that the pacing and the not knowing and the absent God are prayer too.

*

And so is constipation.

When the vegetables and fruit Alice grows are running low and she cannot find any at the markets and our pottage is mostly cereal, my body suffers.

The waste in me moves but will not leave. I am leaden inside, lead that turns in my gut and brings a terrible deep pain which starts after Matins and keeps sleep from me. I cannot think; I light a candle but I cannot read. Eventually I sleep for a short while before rising, unrelieved, to recite Lauds and Prime, with no sense of the meaning only a longing to finish, the words pushed to the sides and suffocated by the heavy fullness that is in me.

Saint Bonaventure, come to my aid now!

I go to my pot. There has to be release. The waste cannot stay in me. I am determined. I have time now before Terce and I will give the time not to study or to contemplation but to my body.

I sit, and push.

Nothing.

I push again. And again. My body protests. I twist my torso as my mother taught me, to help the guts inside release their cumbrance.

Nothing.

And nothing.

Time is passing. Must I rise to pray unrelieved? Sweet Saint Bonaventure, scholar, teacher of contemplation, patron saint of my bowel, come to my aid now!

I push. It hurts. But now there is some movement downwards, slowly, so slowly and the matter is hard. It reaches the doorway of my body and begins to emerge and dear Lord Jesu the pain is terrible. Every push to help the waste leave has me wincing in sharp pain.

I am stuck and now it is time to pray Terce.

So – I pray on my pot. I cannot reach my breviary from where I am perched so I recite what I can remember and when I have reached the end of my memory I repeat the *Pater Noster* and the *Ave Maria*, my prayers spoken in the midst of my bodily distress, my exposed indignity, my unprayerful squatting.

But I do not feel that God is displeased. On the contrary, I can hear Him laughing. Kindly.

Now Terce is finished and I am still stuck, mid-release, no movement, and only pain if I push. My body is aching, cramped and cold on the pot, I have kept Alice with our midday meal away but I cannot keep her away for ever, it has been more than three hours, dear Saint Bonaventure, I am desperate—

I ease the waste from my body with my own hand. Guided by the saint? God is not absent from this unspeakably revolting and relieving action. God does not scorn this work as He does not scorn any work. And afterwards I look at the soil on my hands as I scrub them in plentiful water that Alice heats and brings to me, and I see that it is no different from the soil of the earth. Indeed that is where our waste goes, to fertilise the earth and make things grow. What is there to be revolted by? And I ask Alice to bring me some soil from the garden outside and before their final rinse I wash my hands in damp soil.

I am muddied with earth, part of earth, gardened.

XLII

I am not left to work everything out on my own.

Mother Abbess visits and guides and advises from her years as a woman religious, patiently repeating her words of preparation as their meaning becomes real in my hermit's life, not theory.

The Abbess and you, Thomas my confessor, are alone amongst my visitors in being permitted to speak to me through my squint into the church, sacred portal for Jesu's body at the mass, and mercifully sheltered from the weather. Merciful to me, for it means she can visit without discomfort at any time of the year, and so can you, beloved Thomas, your honest face with its holy purpose attending to my confession or giving me direction through the squint, sitting in the sanctuary, just as you are now. You return weekly in those early years, keeping me steadfast in my calling as it settles in me.

Alice roots herself beside me, strong oak by my slender birch, clever and attentive and busy without disturbing me, guarding my silence from visitors until I am ready to see them. She tends the neglected garden of my predecessor Giles. On the south-west corner of the plot, on the day of my interment, she planted an apple tree. Most of her garden I cannot see, but her tree, already three feet at the time of its translation, is visible from my window, growing beside me.

Father Walter is a support too. I grow fond of him, bumbling his way through mass, often forgetting to bring me communion on the days I receive, which only leaves me hungrier for the next sacred meal. But he is not my anchored companion for long.

It is advent. Today at the mass Father Walter makes even more mistakes than usual and I hear a sigh ripple through the congregation as they endure his inadequate priestliness, wondering if the wafer they worship is truly the body of Jesu since the prayer to consecrate it has been so mangled. I am hungry with fasting and try to be patient. He seats himself with a little grunt at the end of communion, resting his back against the wall, the carved stone niche framing his slumped shoulders, his tilted-forward head, his closed eyes. No doubt he is relieved that his task for today is nearly over.

The silence lengthens. By now Father Walter should have come to the altar to close the mass with a recitation of the beginning of St John's Gospel – *In principio erat Verbum* – In the beginning was the Word – releasing the people back into their lives. But he sits still. I look at him wondering. He is so still, and slumped. I can hear no sound from the congregation. They are waiting, held I think by his strange stillness from simply giving up and leaving, which they have done often enough in the past, accustomed to missing the indulgence granted by hearing this last word of God. But Walter does not move, and neither do they. And finally the little boy server, whom I know now is called Tom, appears in my framed picture of Walter's seated, slumped figure, and goes to him. He reaches to place a hand on his shoulder, and Walter does not respond.

The funeral mass is held the next day.

Robert Grylle becomes priest and stays for a long time and he could not be more different. Precise, vigilant, correct, cold, and later dangerous.

1381–1385

XLIII

A great storm batters the land, tearing the spring buds and leaves from the trees and the trees from the ground. The wind is from the east and does not have a window to my cell to breach, but it gets in anyway and even as I shiver I am pleased beyond measure to find a sprig of apple blossom, five-petalled, translucent white and pale yellow, fastened still to its gnarled little twig, broken, bruised and perfect, delivered to my windowsill in a gust from the garden. Today I touch Alice's apple tree with my hands not just my eyes. The tree itself is sturdy, like Alice, like my cell and this church; we survive the tormenting squalls.

News of Wat Tyler's protest passes to me through those who come for counsel. My visitors take sides, often against, sometimes for. The uprising seems a distraction from painful memories of the pestilence, but reminders are everywhere and the utterly diminished numbers of labourers is one of them. Wat Tyler is demanding just wages for this ragged tail-end army of workers, and he is on his way to London. Even from my anchorage I can feel the pull of his will, the fierce hope he awakens in the breast of those who have not been well treated and who are learning their worth from him. They know they are needed.

Do I favour the rebel workers? My visitors want to know, as though my opinion would determine their fate. I do not say, though nor do I quarrel with the conclusion drawn by some that my silence means I am sympathetic. Who would not sympathise with those who have brought wealth to our lands by their work and enjoyed none of its fruits? On whom a poll tax has now been laid, a tax for simply existing?

They tell me of promises made by the King as he flees the great Tower in London, stormed and taken by bloodthirsty Johanna Ferrour. A woman forcing the King to turn tail! Backed into a corner, he says he will pass new laws to protect the labourers from serfdom, and signs charters to show his good faith. But news comes fast on the heels of this: Wat Tyler has been killed, his murderers rewarded with knighthoods; the King's promises have all been retracted.

Repression only increases the anger that rises over England, and the rebellious numbers swell and pulse out across the land; one pulse brings fighting men to Norwich and the city is assaulted. Alice stays within her room beside my anchorhold. Others seek sanctuary in the church. I sit as still as I can, breathing my prayers, anxious for John and his family. But though the angry work of destruction is close enough for us to hear, no harm comes to this little church. The wave of fury passes through the city and away as the men leave, and silence, full of fear, falls on us all.

Alice ventures out with Father Robert to find food. She returns with stories of some houses destroyed, others left intact: the men were targeting their overlords and knew where to strike. Knowing I would like to be told, she has enquired about John's household, and reassures me that it has been spared. The greater excitement is that Henry, the

Bishop, he to whom I made my vows, is on the march to quell the rebellion and he is striking hard at those who attacked our city.

I hear in fits and starts of the Bishop's battles from my few visitors and from Alice who picks up what can be known locally in her forays for food. Food that is becoming scarcer. We are grateful to have pottage every day and my gut is grateful for the vegetables from Alice's garden. There is little rain to freshen the brackish water, so we drink only ale for safety.

The rebels are swiftly quelled and the city returns to life; the Bishop is seeking fights abroad now. But Alice brings word that the Wycliffites are no longer tolerated as they were, for the nobility are fearful now of the peasants, and it is among the peasants that Wycliffe's teaching flourishes.

The church has been granted authority to bring heretics to trial, she tells me.

I do not heed her, for at this time I do not feel any threat to me from the suspicion of heresy that is slowly growing all around my cell. No more am I pestered by those who think my faith and my calling are invalid. And the bright colours of the visions have faded a little. They do not present themselves in my prayers with their vivid disturbing truths as they have done and I do not believe I am in any danger.

Another year passes and we settle down and carry on as people always do. I am glad that my tranquillity and my chosen way of life have not been unduly shaken by the world's unrest. I hear word that the Abbess has died and I pray diligently for her soul, but I do not miss her. I think I have learned all I needed from her. I am settled in my cell and at peace with my calling. My days are measured and undemanding and, I say this now, Thomas, with the clearer vision of distance, smug. Superior. Superior as those who seek counsel visit and I am able to advise well and see them depart consoled. Superior as I pray so unceasingly in my cell and hear the sounds of the people only once a day coming into the church for holy Office; superior as I hear Father Robert say the mass in his correct unlively manner; superior as the dimpled shallow stutter of public prayer trips uncertainly along beside the deep unruffled calm flow of my own private prayer; superior as I hear the people rustle back out of the church to their busy lives, their troubled lives, and I, glad they have taken their noise with them, continue to meditate in the prevailing quiet. Superior, even when there is undue chatter outside my cell, which irritates me deeply – this should have been a clue, Thomas, a warning – and I think of the inconsiderate people who are heedless of the hermit and her prayer, which they are disturbing, and I think I will pray for them but that does not stop the voices irritating and disturbing me; they should be quiet or go away. But the noise always does pass eventually and I return to my tranquil prayer, for I have chosen Mary's part, the good part, the most important part, have I not? And it shall not be taken from me.

I am a fool.

XLIV

A religious man, Gavin, a youth known for his holiness of life, comes to me for counsel. Or so he has claimed to Alice. His face appears at the external window, his cheekbones standing proud in his gaunt face, blue eyes pale as water, thin hair the colour of sand, pointy nose a-drip. He looks weak, he sounds weak, his voice is unpleasantly high pitched as he names himself,

Ga-vin,

and I nod with condescension, ready to hear his need.

But his eyes are accusing, boldly fixed upon mine. He does not speak of his troubles. His first question hits me with force, it is so unexpected. In a voice that grates and squeaks, he says

How do you know your faith is true, daughter?

My faith?

I am thrown. Before I can answer he continues,

Are your prayers valid? Is your vocation from God? How do you know it is not from your sinful self, from your own pride?

I-I trust—

He does not wait.

How do you know whether you are living your life in selfishness? Reserving to yourself your holiness? Your reputation is growing, daughter,

How dare he call me daughter? This *boy*.

Your reputation is growing and you glory in it

He is working himself into a fury

You glory in it and you are in terrible danger of forgetting Jesu your Saviour because of your pride. What are you doing about it?

I flinch as the sharp darts pierce. Doubt floods my being and I have no protection against him as he questions me and further questions me. Somewhere within I understand that his accusations are against himself and he is casting from him the deep fear that he may be mistaken in his vocation by seeing the same fear in others, in me. But that does not stop the darts of his furious questions piercing me. And I cannot gather my thoughts to respond.

I weep – weep! My tears enrage me as I weakly protest

I know I am unworthy, I am tempted, subject to pride, yes, I do feel pleased with how I am regarded, but I know these dangers, I am trying not to be subject to them, I try to remember my Saviour Jesu . . .

Feeble inarticulate protestations, as though Gavin were my confessor, but he is not, he is a sad creature with a brittle unkind voice, weakness hiding behind aggression; he knows nothing of my life and he is a spiritual infant. And yet I am debased, utterly embarrassed and humiliated by this weedy man. He is pathetic. Why can I summon no power to withstand him?

When he is gone I draw the curtain and sit still, stunned by how quickly and completely my peace has been destroyed by this – this *Ga-vin*. His motives are suspect, his intention distorted and I should not be troubled, but he has reached unerringly into my unsteady soul as though he *knows* it is there, lurking behind my tranquil exterior, and he has torn my tranquil exterior which has been so long in the making, torn it from me like a robe made of rags, made of nothing. It dissolved at his swift harsh touch, and the pathetic person I really am is exposed.

To this day, Thomas, I do not know whether he had come for counsel or whether, as I thought immediately after he had gone, he was sent by the Bishop to test my faith, for holy church was growing zealous in using her new powers to bring heretics to trial. But I never saw him again.

XLV

I cannot find the rags of my self-confidence to wrap around me again and I tell Alice I can see no more visitors that day. I creep like the naked pathetic thing I am through my prayers, grateful beyond measure that I can hide in my cell, that none can see me. But in the night the cell presses upon me unbearably and I pace its narrow confines like the angry wild creature I thought had long since been tamed. I cannot sleep. There is no solace, not in God who is absent, not in the beads, not in repeating the *Pater Noster*, whose words turn to dust in my mouth and my mind and do not come alive again. Nothing I have used in the past to steady my soul has the least effect. I do not understand how one person for whom I feel no respect can undo me so completely. But he has. He has stripped me naked, my clothes are gone, and I am nothing without them.

The next day brings no respite. I am weary to my bones, heavy-eyed from lack of sleep, without appetite for food or prayer, sore in body and spirit. I lack all strength to help myself but a voice speaks in me not to seek your aid, Thomas, my confessor and guide, nor Felicia's – not yet. My nakedness shames me. I want to regain my tranquillity and reclothe myself before I speak to you. But my garments remain lost to me. They have disappeared with the prayer of which I thought they were made, of which they *were* made: but the prayer was shallow and for show, and its departure has revealed the weak hypocrite that I am.

I sleep only fitfully this following night, my dreams tormented by laughing fiends. I awaken to face afresh my sham holiness. I am ashamed to pray the Hours, ashamed to present the souls of others to God, ashamed to show myself to visitors as though I have anything of truth or value to offer. I fulfil the day's tasks only because I do not know what else I should do. I eat almost nothing, and again the night is troubled.

In the morning I am dull-eyed and the day unfolds as miserably as before, flat and repetitive and meaningless, except that Alice tells me Isabel, whom I have not seen for a year, is at my window! I am so relieved. She will not judge me, I can say something of my woe, she will help me laugh *Ga-vin* into nothingness. I know she will comfort me.

But she is different today. She sits at the window, her colour high, words tumbling from her before she has even greeted me or asked me how I fare.

> Dearest Julian, I am so glad to see you. I have so much to tell you! I could not come before now, the uprising made it unsafe for nobles to be abroad and we had trouble enough with our own land and people. Then William fell ill and . . . and . . .
>
> Julian, my beloved William died.

I raise my tired eyes to hers, trying to summon sympathy. No words come, but Isabel is too intent on what she is telling me to notice.

He has been dead for three months and I have mourned him deeply. I loved him and I miss him. And I do not like being dowager. I am no longer in charge of my great home and I am interfering too much. I make my nephew and his wife, the new Earl and Countess, mad with my meddling.

Still I have nothing to say, and Isabel continues,

I am less and less able to distract myself with hunting and riding and archery: their appeal is diminishing and my body is not as fit as it was for these pastimes. But I realise that hunting no longer draws me because I want to work on my soul, not my body.

William's death has turned my mind to other things. Holy things.

I have been reading, dear Julian, Boethius's *Consolation*, and he has made me see how empty and meaningless are my high position and worldly power and wealth.

She looks at me, I think noticing my weary eyes and my silence, and her words carry more emphasis.

It is a *marvellous* book.

And Julian . . .

My dear, dear friend, you have taught me so much, you have shown me by your words and your example where I should next place myself.

She stops.

I – I have decided to join the canonesses in Campsey Ash.

The words come out in a rush and she does not wait to read my face.

I have been supporting the community for many years and I went to see them after William died to ask for their prayers for his soul. When I entered the house I felt straightaway that I had come home. I spoke to the Mother Prioress that day, and I have been seeing her ever since, exploring what my heart now longs for, and I do believe, Julian, I do believe that God is calling me to this life and now I want nothing more.

At last she stops speaking.

I do not move. I have no smile or words of encouragement for Isabel. All I can think is that I will not see her again. But she misinterprets my silence, and says quickly

Do not imagine I will leave you unresourced.

There is enough and more for us all. Oh, my dear friend, tell me you are pleased, tell me you understand, tell me you believe I can do this!

I force my face to assume a smile. And discover that as I push the sides of my mouth towards my ears, the feeling of the smile emerges and now I truly am smiling. I forget my pain and loss, and my starved soul receives the new deep joy that shines from Isabel.

I am; I do; you can.

And our eyes rest upon each other with warmth.

But afterwards, when she is gone, I sob till my heart is empty.

Alice tells me Isabel has left a gift for me and would I like to see it? I refuse, thinking it will be some cheerful unnecessary food or frippery.

Just two days later, Alice asks if we could speak. She is not excited, her colour is not high, she is steady as an oak tree, as she always is. But her words bring havoc in their wake.

Mistress, I have taken a decision to seek the life of a hermit myself.

Alice!

How could you? How could you.

I stand still but within I am falling apart. Still, but trembling, a too-slender failing birch tree whose roots are loosened, whose leaves are dying and falling from dry branches, who could be blown down by the slightest tremor of wind, while Alice the sturdy oak stands tall and strong, with deep roots and powerful branches and green growing leaves that spread and shelter all creatures, most of all me, Alice, most of all me.

I stand still and tremble as she continues to speak.

> This decision has been long in coming and is not made lightly. I
> did not think I would leave you. But I cannot ignore the call in
> me. I have been seeking counsel with Father Robert, I did not
> want to trouble you, and anyway I have learned so much from you
> already in serving you all this time.

> Now you know my heart, mistress, will you add your support to
> those who have already written to the Bishop?

Though you have lived so close beside me all this time, Alice, I have
not noticed the change in you. In my smug tranquillity I did not
see you. But I see you now and you have made up your mind as
surely as you have done before. This time to a life without me.

How could you leave at just this time, when I am more in need of
your service than I have ever been since entering my anchorhold?
When Isabel has only just left me? When we still have to struggle to
find enough food? How will I cope? I cannot bear the thought of
another coming in your place to know me so intimately. My disobedi-
ent gut! There is none who could serve so well as you, you who have
known me all my life. And . . . I love you with all my heart.

I say none of this out loud.

Again the misunderstanding that I am concerned about money.

> You know I have means, she says. My family have written to say
> they will support me.

Alice.

My voice is low and unsteady.

I do not think I can keep my vows without you.

I have spoken truth at last. Humble, contrite admission of my utter weakness, my utter dependence upon the simple service of others. I who believed I chose the good part, Mary's part, loved above all others by Jesu, superior I! Live on my empty prayers? I could not last for one moment without my Martha's work, my Alice's work. And now my Martha is seeking Mary's part, and must abandon me.

Alice looks briefly alarmed but speaks kindly and warmly.

I know you, mistress. I know you have strength which even you do not see in your intense love for God. You have shown me for so long how to live a holy, secluded life. You have nothing to fear, mistress, while I have everything to learn when I go.

And she says,

The hermitage will not be ready for some months, a year perhaps, so there is plenty of time to train a new servant and prepare, both of us, for the parting.

But I cannot find solace in her words. I do not recognise the woman she claims I am; I do not hear that I may have as much as a year till she leaves. I just hear that Alice too is deserting me. And I feel that all my comfort is being taken from me at a time when I have no means to bear it.

*

And then. You, Thomas. An unexpected visit, not at our allocated time.

You *do* notice my heavy eyes and my cheeks' pallor.

> Daughter, you are not at ease. Do you wish to tell me what is in your heart?

I shake my head. I am alarmed at your visit and I want to know why you are here. If I start to speak of my loss and my despair and my helplessness, I will not stop until I am a puddle of mere nothing, and you do not look as though you have the time.

> Julian. I am sorry you are not well because I have news, news of my departure.

You stop at my sharp, indrawn breath. Your face is sorry, and worried.

> My Abbot has assigned me the role of chantry priest in . . . in Aylsham. It is some distance from here.

I slowly lower my forehead and rest it on my hands, which are clasping the sill between us.

No. You cannot do this to me. You cannot do this, God!

I dimly hear your voice telling me again how sorry you are, how you are bound by your vow of obedience and you have no choice, that you have found me another confessor whom I can trust, but the roar in my own heart is too loud to make sense of what you say, the roar in my heart and the hammering of my fists on God's heart: how can I survive this hateful trilogy of loss? How could You remove every crutch when I cannot stand unaided? I have nothing, I am nothing, I am abandoned. Abandoned in the desert. Helpless.

I look up as you make to rise, shaking your head and running your hand over your tonsure, agitated, promising to return with the name of my new confessor, with more words of comfort. And you disappear from the frame of my squint.

Lord without mercy!

I turn my gaze upon myself and tear my soul to shreds. I am so ashamed. I thought I was strong. I thought I was supporting Isabel, and Alice, even you sometimes, Thomas. But now, as you leave me one by one, I discover I have no strength of my own. How easy it is for this feeble anchoress hiding in her cell to maintain the semblance of holiness, the appearance of interiority! How I have been fooled, lulled into complacency!

I become like a hurt animal curled up in the darkness, suffering silently, bleeding grief and shame.

*

I do not know, Thomas, how important is this time of darkness and unknowing and unhappiness. I just live through it. A membrane had been slowly thickening around me, a thick skin made of my holy life with its time laid out for prayer and counsel and, yes, even the visions, though they had receded and I had not paid heed. I was too busy giving the impression of meaning where there was none. This interior life I had sought: it was all exterior only.

My wounds, those wounds like Saint Cecilia's that I asked for as a child, that have carried me through life, brought me the visions and brought me here, are covered with thick scar tissue. And now they are breaking open again.

XLVI

The toughened membrane does not shed itself so easily with only my solitary inadequate penitence to soften it.

I do not know Roger Reed, my new confessor, who looks as different from you as it is possible to be, dear Thomas, except that he too wears the black Benedictine habit: he is so tall that on his arrival I see only his belted torso in the squint, and that is spare indeed. When he sits I see eyes set far back in a fine-shaped head, their light shining like torches in a tunnel. He says very little but he listens. I can speak only haltingly to him, as I feel my penitence but cannot give voice to it. I suffer it in a fog of unknowing, having to trust that it is God's will and that the fog will pass. Roger does not try to dispel the fog. He listens.

Three years of painstaking practice in my seclusion have come to nothing. I thought I was building confidence and experience and good habits: I was building a wall, a second wall within the walls of my cell.

It takes time to accept that this inner cell wall is of no value, this membrane made of hard, hard work that I have claimed for myself without realising it. It takes time because I do not want to see it go. I cannot believe that all I have achieved thus far is of no use. Surely I need it, for myself and my own prayer, and for those who seek my advice, thinking me wise? And I do not want to prove that vile man, *Ga-vin*, was right.

Sarah arrives from Isabel's household, not wanting to stay when her beloved mistress is herself departing, Sarah who is very short, very stout, with a brown weathered face, who is soft, and kind, and a quick learner from Alice, whose room she shares for two months before Alice leaves.

Which she does. Which she does.

I tell myself that Sarah's expectation of my holiness means I must keep at my now-empty prayers, and so does Father Robert's meticulous attention to his own religious duty carried out in the church so close alongside me. But in truth I keep going because I am terrified to let go of my carapace. All through Sarah's apprenticeship with Alice and for months thereafter, I keep my established routine, looking again and again for life in my old habits. There is none. God does not awaken the soul in me to feel, and I cannot awaken myself. I try, but it is like shaking the shoulders of a corpse.

I am so desolate. Isabel and Alice and you, Thomas, have abandoned me. The Abbess is dead and her successor is as yet unknown to me. I *have* to support myself with my own prayers; if I cannot then I truly am a dead thing. Dead, and buried in this anchorhold from which I have no escape.

And so I keep shaking the corpse of my vocation with my empty prayers, for what else can I do?

*

And then one evening, as on my knees I chant the final words of Compline,

In manus tuas Domine, commendo spiritum meum
Into Thy hands, O Lord, I commend my spirit

I give up. I let go. Of everything.

XLVII

I stay there for a long time in quiet, light, fearless, blissful emptiness.

He hath no virtue, nor is He virtue, nor light, nor does He live, nor is He life, nor is He substance, nor age, nor time, nor is there any understandable touching of Him, nor is He cunning, nor truth, nor kingdom, nor wisdom, not one, not unity, not Godheed, not goodness, nor is He spirit as we understand spirit, nor sonhead, nor fatherhead, nor any other thing known by us, nor of any that has been, nor is there any way by reason or understanding to come unto Him.

These words of Dionysius sound in my mind in the unformed and light-hearted days that follow, when I cannot see why I should pick up my vocation again since it has brought me only rigid and false separation, and whether I pray or not God is unaffected. For God is everywhere at this time. I am flooded by God. Sarah is confused but mercifully unquestioning in the face of my laughing freedom as I abandon the Offices, sleep when I want, ask for food three or four times a day, or don't eat at all. I am flooded by God and nothing else matters. I no longer kneel but sit for hours in contemplation, in simple bliss, with no words, and that is all there is and it is all I need.

*

It is spring, it is night, I am awake, a gentle rain falls.

I quietly approach the window of my cell that is opposite Sarah's door and listen for her. I can hear her snoring.

I draw back the curtain of the visitors' window

and climb onto its ledge

and I go outside.

XLVIII

I keep close to my cell wall, the stone rough under my unaccustomed fingers as I feel my way carefully round it to the garden that is hidden in the shadows between the east wall of my cell and the church.

I am out of my grave now. In the safety of this tucked-away garden, I step out from the wall and turn my face to the sky. The soft rain stipples and patters on my starved skin, skin so fine that it feels transparent and were the rain not so gentle I am certain it would penetrate and soak my thirsty soul, but my soul is drinking anyway, drinking with my body as it receives this delicious watery blessing. My eyes are closed to feel the rain on my eyelids, my hands are open to feel the rain on my palms. I become aware through my bare feet of the garden's friable soil where food is growing. My toes curl around the damp muddiness and my feet shift and move and lift up and now I am moving and swaying, my face still turned up to the sky and the soft rain, my eyes still closed, and I open and close my palms, and move my arms, and lift my legs and I can feel my binding death-shroud fall from me, and I dance! Leaping around the garden, spinning and swaying, faster and faster as silent laughter bubbles up within me, opening my mouth to set the laughter free, tasting the rain in my mouth, sticking out my tongue to drink more of its sweetness, stamping my feet in the soft silent earth, throwing my arms about above my head, wildness and joy and freedom in me and all about me

and then the rain stops and the dance slows and my movements become sedate and dignified, stepping lightly around the little garden, still rejoicing but gravely.

A light wind rises and the clouds part and I cease my dance. I turn my face to the sky again as bright stars and brighter planets and the cold sickle moon show themselves to me.

My gaze deepens into the far distant heavens. It is so vast.

And my soul settles.

It is so vast and I am so little, a tiny speck in the universe. I am not nothing and I am not everything and there is so much universe and I have seen it fragile in the palm of my hand. And my beloved brother Jesu, my loving mother God, has asked me if He could have suffered more for the pain that it suffers, has pleaded to know if I am apaid.

I am. And I have so much more still to learn.

The sky blurs as my tears start. I am very quiet. It is time to go back to my anchorhold.

And very quietly, I make my way back, and I turn to my altar and return to my knees before my beloved, in gratitude, in simplicity, in supplication because my work is not finished and I have more to learn.

XLIX

In the morning I see muddy footprints marking the rushes on my floor, and then I see my nightshift thrown over my chair, still damp, and covered with mud splatters, clearly visible from Sarah's window. And I realise the garden, Sarah's garden, will be thoroughly trampled.

Sarah does not say a word to me about it, but that afternoon Felicia appears. The only friend who might understand what is happening to me, who would not betray me and to whom I might listen with respect, has come to visit me today. I have not seen her for months and months. It cannot be a coincidence.

Wise Sarah.

Dionysius's words are true, says Felicia, but you are in this life and you should not abandon your calling. Yes, it is limited, it will not on its own bring you to God: nothing can; God can. Continue in your work because it is valuable. Continue in your work without ambition or pride. But continue. You will find you still need to praise God, thank God, be sorry before God.

With your quiet attentiveness in prayer and conversation you will become as a still lake. Love herself will come and find her reflection in you.

Then Felicia smiles her rare, radiant smile.

It is good to see you back, dear sister Julian. I have missed you.

And I bow my head in shame once more at the thick skin I had grown around myself, which had taken me from my friends.

*

I pick up my duties again. But everything is to be learned afresh. Every word of the Office, every consecration at the mass, every moment of contemplation, every encounter at my window becomes a new thing, unfamiliar, strange. I do not know how to be with these practices, I am awkward, foolish, stumbling – and utterly compelled.

My cell becomes enormous. The world when I went outside is in here now; it entered the cell with me when I chose to re-enter. And I am moving in this enormous new world like a babe just emerged from the womb. I am pale and unformed, almost transparent, and I do not try to build protection around my feeble soul. I allow myself to be porous, pregnable, I take that risk. And my cell feels porous too: the world outside that had so irritated and disturbed me, the stuttering prayers of the church's congregation, the noisy chatter of people passing by, the foolish truthful words of those who seek my counsel, they are somehow no longer outside. They are within my cell, they are with me, with me not as inferiors but as my teachers and I am their pupil.

Isabel's parting gift was no frippery, but the book that turned her own eyes inwards: *The Consolation of Philosophy* newly translated into English by Geoffrey Chaucer. Like me, Boethius was in a cell, though for him it was not sought. He was an honourable man in high public office who had been betrayed by his enemies, convicted and imprisoned. He lost everything that he had worked for all his life. He sought to bring virtue to the world of public service and the world spat him out. A good man brought low. And out of his bewilderment and deep unhappiness came words; in his cell he wrote his *Consolation*. He wrote of being visited by Philosophy in the form of a woman, who with her gentle guidance and wise reasoning changed his perception, so that he saw how truth and goodness and happiness would never be found in worldly gain or power or wealth or reputation. By his writing, his perception is changed, and so is that of his readers.

It is a text of loving clarity, Thomas. It speaks to every heart, not just that of the contemplative. And as, childlike, I slowly read and reflected, it brought me to a deeper understanding of where Love may be found.

That the world with stable faith
Varieth accordable changes,
That the contrarious quality of elements
Holds among themselves lasting alliance.
That Phoebus the sun with his golden chariot
Bringeth forth the rosene day;
That the moon had commandment over the nights
Which nights Hesperus the evening star hath brought;
That the sea, greedy to flow, constraineth with a certain end
   his floods
So that it is not leveful to stretch his broad terms or bounds
   upon the earth,

That is to say to cover all the earth.
All this accordance of things is bounden with love
That governeth earth and sea,
And He hath also commandment to the heavens.

And if this love slaked the bridles,
All things that now hold them together
Would make a battle continually and strive to destroy the
    fashion of this world
The which they now live in accordable faith by fair movings.

This love holds together peoples
Joined with an holy bond,
And knitteth sacrament of marriages of chaste loves,
And love promulgates laws to true fellows.
O joyful were mankind
If this love that governeth heaven governeth your hearts!

I am no longer Mary, pure and withdrawn from the world.

The mighty dynamic universe is knit together by love that might
govern our hearts also. Without knowing how it may be so, I discover
my deep interiority here. Here in what is and what may be between
us. All of us.

1385–1388

L

I have been grateful for Father Robert's precision and competence in saying the Office and the mass, but his elegant liturgy is becoming too correct. His voice at the altar sounds strangled. He is growing in severity.

He is not certain how to deal with me, has never been certain. Roger my confessor tells me that although there are more recluses in Norwich now, and some of them women, Robert has not served in a church with an anchorite before and he is uncomfortable with my presence. He deals with me by ignoring me, except when he brings me the body of Jesu at the masses when I receive, no more than fifteen times in a year. He does not come to my window to speak to me and see how I fare. I pray for him but I cannot support him otherwise because he remains out of reach.

And now I think it is just as well. There is a new rigidity upon him that I learn to recognise. It is stealing upon all those who come to seek counsel. The truth of what is in our hearts is harder to speak and the love that comes from that truth cannot flow, because the truth does not flow. There is fear and then more fear in the eyes of my visitors. They know they must not go against holy church, and holy church is stricter now.

Today a young man comes to me, his eyes eager.

Dame Julian, I want your counsel. I feel the pull of vocation, not to the enclosed life but to a mendicant life, preaching God's word in the world. I feel such love rising in me for all humanity, and I feel words rising in me too . . .

He stops.

What is it?

The words that rise in me . . .

He stops again.

I wait, puzzle turning to dismay: I recognise this obstructing power.

The words to speak of God's glory, they are almost impossible to find, are they not?

God will always defy our attempts to enclose Him in words, though words are all we have.

But when you cannot find the words, and then the words are given to you . . .

Yes?

He whispers now.

They are not always as holy church would have us speak.

How do you know?

The young man looks around carefully to ensure no one is by. He leans closer to my window.

I was overheard in the street by a priest in the Bishop's household, who admonished me. I can't even remember what I was saying, but it was not as holy church teaches said the priest, and he told me to be silent. I do not know what was wrong in my words. I sought no difference from holy church. But if I have to guard my words and check them before they leave my heart they dry up. I have to allow the words and I do not know what they will be before they emerge. And if they emerge wrong, I place myself and my loved ones in danger.

The lively rising spirit in a man encounters holy church and is crushed not encouraged.

And today, a woman with frowning lines etched on her brow and thin, pinched lips. She puts her question. I do not remember what it is, Thomas, because my memory of this meeting is only the way I myself am silenced. Not because I am bidden, but because wisdom deserts me. Words shrivel as they rise into the light of this woman's disfavour. I understand that what stops in me is a reflection of what is in the heart of my visitor, but though I can see this, I am powerless to do anything about it, as though a lock has been put upon me by the other and only she has the key, but she can't see it. All I can do is gently attend and not allow anything hard to sit in me that would hit against the hardness of her ear, in her mouth, in her heart.

Her disfavour has the strength of holy church behind it. It is not she but the priests who commend the examination of all words to ensure they are orthodox, and she obeys, and there is no life in our exchange.

But nor is there love in this exchange with a follower of Wycliffe who has all the ardent vigour of William and Adam and none of their gentleness. He would have me cease my prayers for the dead, cease my worship of the risen Christ in the consecrated bread, cease my prayers before statues of Jesu and Mary his mother.

It is idolatry, he says in a fierce whisper; you are worshipping gross matter not God.

He questions my celibate life: he does not believe I am chaste.

It is not possible, he says, peering suspiciously in at my window, and certainly not for your maid.

He speaks angrily. I listen and watch anger rise in me also, but with an effort I let it flow through me and out, hoping that may soften his anger too.

He is not wise but some of his quarrels with holy church have merit. And yet holy church, instead of receiving the objections with wisdom and love, sets herself up in opposition and demands that we take sides, and show we take sides by our words, not what is in our hearts, and judges those words.

Aside from prayer, words are all we who are recluses have with which to serve others and they are being made into weapons.

There have always been those who believe the text of my visions is evidence I am a Wycliffite, and this now matters, increasingly so. Confessor Roger says he is hearing this said of me, that I am a heretic. They should read the words, I tell him. But hearsay is not based upon evidence. The simple existence of the text is enough to cast suspicion upon me: words from a woman who should not take it upon herself to speak of such things in English to describe a God who belongs in Latin, to the men of holy church.

LI

Bishop Henry's crusade in Flanders against the false Pope Clement and his war with King Richard against Scotland have ended in failure. He has gained nothing but a fearful reputation, and he has returned to Norwich bristling. His blood is up, has always been up: he declares his faith in God by fighting and knows no other means to tell it. And now there are no more wars abroad he turns his fierce eye upon us.

The followers of Wycliffe are openly declared heretics, and so is anyone who does not strictly follow the teaching of holy church, every one of them branded a Lollard, a mutterer against authority. Nothing has changed for the peasants since Wat Tyler's failed uprising, and they still seek justice from the King, but their efforts blur into complaints against the church's power. And so sedition and heresy become one; ordinary people are suspected of Lollardy just because they are ordinary, and no one is safe.

Holy church has power to bring heretics to trial and Bishop Henry uses that power mercilessly. He will not rest till the last Lollard is gone from his diocese. He is actively seeking, and seeing everywhere, heretic souls. It is not safe to speak in case speech errs against

King or holy church and is overheard and reported. But suspicion sows its own seeds and mute rebellion rises, hidden in close-drawn wimples and hoods. And so an enemy is created out of nothing, out of fear.

LII

It is Lent. Sarah has returned from the market and is preparing our meal. She is making much more noise than is her custom, and I lift my head from my prayer, wondering what has upset her.

She brings me food. Her face is deeply flushed and her hands are trembling as she passes the bowl with its meagre Lenten pottage, oats and vegetables only, through the window.

What is it, Sarah?

She looks at me imploringly, tears standing in her eyes.

What is it?

A moment of silence. Then, abruptly, she asks

What do Lollards eat?

I am taken aback.

I – I think they do not keep the fasts of holy church. Is that what you mean?

Yes! That is why some men stopped me as I was returning from market. They demanded to see what was in my basket. They were so rude, they rummaged and rummaged – the basket is small enough and there was little enough in it, but they seemed not to be satisfied, certain that I was hiding something . . .

Meat? I say. If you had meat in your basket it would prove you and I were Lollards.

We both laugh. We would not eat meat in Lent but we do not eat it at all now Isabel is enclosed. But Sarah grows serious again.

The men told me they were the Bishop's agents and had great power. They knew I was your servant, they said, and they wanted me to tell them about you, how you spend your day and most importantly who visits you at your window. And then . . . Mistress! They told me I should tell them who visits you in the future, and I should listen to your conversations and report them. I told them I could never do that, and . . . they offered me money.

Sarah hangs her head. I try to keep my voice calm.

Did you take it?

Sarah looks up at me, her face distraught.

No!

She hesitates under my enquiring gaze.

I was tempted. A little bit tempted.

She hangs her head again. I spend time calming her and praising her for her forbearance. I tell her she must stay strong and not reveal the visitors or conversations, not because they are heretical, I say, but because they are private, sacredly so, and she must protect their privacy.

If you cannot do that, Sarah, you must leave my service.

I will not! she protests, weeping

and I choose to believe her. She showed good judgement in seeking Felicia's help in the early days of her service to me. But I realise the risks she faces and how much I depend upon her loyalty and the strength of her will. I say,

Whenever you are so accosted, you must tell me exactly what the men said, what they asked of you, and what you said in reply.

And, Sarah, I rely upon you to bring my visitors to me, whoever they are. Do not take it upon yourself to decide whom I should see, and whom I may not see. That will only raise more suspicion. I must receive who comes.

We will both be careful.

I seek the counsel of my confessor Roger, whom by now I trust absolutely.

You are right to be careful, he says. Sarah is loyal but they will keep pestering her. I have learned that the Bishop is suspicious of the growing number of recluses in Norwich. He believes that you are harbouring Lollard thoughts in your secret cells and spreading Lollard poison in your counsel of others and he is determined to cleanse the city of such filth.

Julian, he is speaking of breaking down the bricked-up doors and searching your cells himself.

LIII

I draw back from the squint in shock. This is unthinkable. Were the Bishop to enter my cell he would make a mockery of my vows, the very same vows that I made to him. And yet if he demanded to do so I could not refuse him because the vows I made to him include obedience. To him. It feels like a clever trap, basely laid by a prelate to whom all turn for leadership in their faith.

I am more shocked at the Bishop's base zeal than I am fearful of his persecution. For all the questions I have of holy church, I have never abandoned her, and Henry is a Bishop of holy church. A man of God, leading us all from his oh-so-high-up seat in the cathedral. I have granted him purity of motive even when his acts have been wrongly chosen. His call to serve God I never questioned. But this wily threat is so contrary to that call, my belief in him shatters.

In the splinters of my belief I find broken shards of holy church herself.

I become wary. Of everything. I do not try to handle the splinters and the shards, they are too sharp, they will damage further and may destroy what is true. I pray, and wait. I see every visitor but I am careful as I speak with them, for I do not know if they are true or have come to trap me into saying that which would convict me of heresy. Now my skill of discernment is needed more than ever. I can usually tell if someone is lying, if I am given time to listen and not speak myself, but so often the spying visitors ask me questions requiring answers. So I never fail to honour holy church in my counsel and to urge the questioner to keep faith.

I do not lie when I say these things. I will not handle the splinters and shards. Holy church is not false.

Holy church is not false. I tell myself this.

Sometimes I hear men whispering with Father Robert in the church. And now, suddenly, Robert's face is at my squint after mass today.

How fare you, Dame Julian?

His bit-back voice is not kind, his pointy nose intrudes into my cell, his lanky hair swinging forward as he leans into my privacy.

Do you have all you need?

This is not concern for my welfare. This is spying. And he makes his enquiries and looks into my cell every day from then on. I would like to ask him if he is being paid for his trouble but I bite my tongue and answer his questions patiently and make myself biddable. At every exchange my dislike of him grows.

*

The people's fear hardens to anger. The Bishop redoubles the zeal of his persecution. I watch and listen from my porous cell.

In my mind I understand that the zealous anger is born not of the truth of holy church but of the grief the pestilence brought upon us. It was devastating, but no one speaks of it now. I do not believe that the grief has abated. I feel it in myself, in my own loss which stays with me and always will. Our children, who are our hope, were taken from us. Our hope. But we have suppressed our grief.

Perhaps, I think, we cannot bear the realisation that we were helpless to avoid the pitiless scourge, that our prayers and our tears and our clever physic were powerless. So we ask why it happened and holy church has told us that the pestilence was God's will. But this is empty reasoning, without heart, explaining nothing, comforting no one, only distancing God in a cloud of wrath.

Holy church does not speak of Christ's wounds as God's wounds, of God knowing our pain as His own.

Instead of giving ourselves time, time to grieve and time to learn what the pain and the loss and the helplessness mean, we have turned our faces towards other things that we think we can control, like sedition and heresy, and let the fury that was in truth grief grow in us, against each other.

I feel impotent in the face of the fiends that are in holy church and are stalking the land, eating men's souls. But the impotence has its own power because resistance to the anger only breeds more anger and I can resist nothing. I have been stripped of my facade of holiness to protect and pretend. No outer skin. No thick membrane. A pale newborn soul, utterly porous to the world and to God, almost transparent but not without the sense to deflect evil when it comes poking at my cell. I have not before prayed so deeply; nor have I found such a quick wit, a ready laugh, storms of cleansing tears. And a new, restful confidence, not in me but in love. Steadfast love.

LIV

There is no end of love. I can explore and discover more and more of what is in this world, what is in me, and however much the priests tell me otherwise, I need not fear what I will find. When I veil my window I can breathe again and the words that are in my mind and my heart can flow freely again, believing despite what holy church says that I am so loved by God that whatever I find in me, whatever comes from me, however stumbling and mistaken, is received lovingly as a mother receives all that her child brings to her in good faith. A mother who suffers untold pain to bring her child to birth and feels in herself every movement of her child's pain and joy. I see this. My visions show me this.

I must whisper, Thomas.

Holy church is no loving mother.

In my anchored cell, cleaving so close, I can feel holy church move, shaken by challenge, shrinking into herself from fear, hardening herself against opposition. I feel this because I am entirely attached.

Holy church is anchored to me as surely as I am anchored to her and I think: I will try, I will *try*, to embody and speak of the love that will not abandon us, that is patient, as Saint Paul teaches, that is kind.

And in this time of my impotent open thin-skinned porosity, when the people and all the earth are suffering and the sharp temper of holy church only increases their pain, when evil abounds despite the many, many good men and women striving otherwise, the visions return to me in full force. They pour themselves out upon me, sometimes in order, sometimes all at once, flooding my mind and heart with all that I saw, and I see more now, and much of it is mysterious, unsettling, other than the teaching of holy church, but it is what I have, what was given to me.

And then one day, as clear as a bell, I hear these words:

Wouldst thou apprehend thy Lord's meaning in this thing?

Wit it well.

Love was His meaning.

You will understand more and again more of what you have seen in your visions but you will never, ever know other than the love from which they came, of which they tell.

Love is our Lord's meaning. In this love God has done all work; and in this love God shares and makes all this pain profitable to us; and in this love our life is, always.

In this love God granted me visions and the visions *mean* love and they are for everyone.

Love is His meaning. My mind and heart are completely open, the wounds bleeding afresh. For I perceive this everlasting unbreakable love and I understand that holy church, whatever she cries to us now, is also in this love and I do not stop loving holy church. And I understand, dimly, that by not abandoning holy church even as the visions teach me holy church is wrong to condemn and accuse and banish and burn, by *not* abandoning her, my wounds will keep bleeding and my understanding will grow. My deep interiority is here, where we meet. I cannot turn my back.

I am anchored; holy church is anchored to me. And I am also free.

And even as the threat of the Bishop's intrusion hangs over me and the danger of being taken for a heretic has never before been so great, I understand that I have to write down the visions as they are showing themselves to me now. Even though, already suspect for my words, I court greater danger by writing more. Even though the words may not be understood; worse, could be deliberately read as potential fodder for the heretic's court. Even though I may have to hide them, therefore, and cannot be certain that they will ever be read, I still have to write them down. For no one. For everyone.

LV

The Bishop does not break into my cell. But his men come openly now, not pretending to seek counsel any more, but to look: through the visitors' window, through Sarah's window though she tries to stop them intruding on the narrow gap between her cell and mine – her sharp-gentle words of protest break upon them like pretty baubles and they laugh at her – and even through the window in the church, kept holy for the receiving of the body of Jesu and for confession. They bid me stand away and they gaze without apology, rudely penetrating every corner of my sanctuary with their prurient eyes. But they do not enter. And they cannot see into my soul.

1388–1392

LVI

The cloud of suspicion, the foolhardiness of the enterprise, the hopelessness that the words will ever be read, serve only to make me more determined. Now the words that are in me about the visions are like a huge child ready and impatient to be born.

Only I don't know how to do it. I might have tried telling the words again to you, dear Thomas, but you are in Aylsham and rarely visit and I do not know how many words there will be nor how long it would take to recount them. There is none other I would entrust with the task of writing them down save Felicia. I whisper to her of my resolve and ask if she would help but she shakes her head.

It would not be safe, she says.

She is right. Nor would it have been safe for you. I would be speaking out loud to either of you – you in the church and only when Father Robert was away, and that would arouse suspicion; Felicia through my window to the world where we would be easily overheard, and she easily overcome if any sought to take from her the words she would be writing at my dictation. Nor, I realise, would it be easy to write out in the open.

There is only myself. And as I lay aside my fears that I will not be up to the task and I accept its responsibility, I see how the choice I made for an enclosed life in a room of my own has always been for this. Not just the undisturbed solitude I needed to bring the truth of the visions to light in my contemplation, gently, exploringly, without fear of being misunderstood and condemned. But to do so with pen and ink, so that others may share their light. My cell is secret. I can write when the church is empty. I can hide my work from prying eyes the rest of the time. None need know.

But how should I write? In Latin? Most books of spiritual learning are in Latin and my words would be held in greater regard by scholars if they were Latin words. And it would be safer, for no Lollard would write Latin. But you, Thomas, you did not write down what I said to you fifteen years ago in Latin. I did not speak with Jesu in Latin and he did not speak to me in Latin, though I hardly know the language in which he did speak, only that I understood it plainly and I still do. If I wrote in Latin I would be translating the words from the visions into a strange tongue and that would change their meaning.

But still, I muse further, the visions are new things and they need new words to tell them, pressed from the experience, bursting newborn from a new seeing. A new language? No, not that. They will be hard enough to describe fully, and I can only trust myself to find the words I will need in English, for with this tongue I have many, many words and I have few indeed in Latin. And the visions are not for the prelates, too full of learning to hear. Nor are they arguments to persuade scholars by proof the existence or the love of God, which lawyerly Latin might force them to be. They are just what I saw and what I see more and more, falling upon me like the pellets of Jesu's blood, the rain on the eaves, flooding me like the broad water rising and flooding the land. They are not arguments, they are showings, to be shown, to be shown to all, for they are *for* all, all my fellow Christians, my fellow people, all. Including the prelates and the fallen. The fallen prelates.

I am seeing my way forward.

In my writing I will become transparent so the words themselves can be encountered directly by the readers, as I directly encountered Jesu, and the words will only evoke the encounter so the readers see Jesu not I, heavens above not I, and the words will not take the reader away into intellectual constructs like other writings that build scaffolding around God for us to climb so we can inspect God as though God were an object of our fascination not life charged through us, not love which is life brought in us by God who loves us, who cares. Who cares. The words will evoke care in their readers as the visions evoke care in me.

So I will write in English, pressing new words from this beautiful plain language spoken by all. Not courtly French to introduce God politely. Not church Latin to construct arguments. English to show Love as she is. Even though it is not safe to do so.

LVII

It is summer and the light is strong still between Vespers and Compline when Father Robert is not in the church. This becomes the time for writing. As the seasons turn and the evenings become too dark, I write in the mornings when Father Robert is absent. I find some time to write every day.

Sarah, brought straightaway into my confidence for I could not do this without her, keeps watch all the time I am writing so I have time to hide it if he, or anyone else, appears unexpectedly.

At the beginning Felicia brings me a copy of your text, Thomas, as an aid to my memory, and a wax tablet and stylus so that I can easily erase words if they are not apt.

I fill the tablet with a list of the showings so that I have a form to my book and my readers will know the shape of what is to come. I have no wish to erase a word, and I wish the words to be in my book. Now that I have started, more words are pressing, hurrying at me to emerge and be written. I need parchment, a lot of it, and I plead with Felicia to tell the others our secret and to help provide the means to write. She smiles with delight and very soon, hidden in a basket under a cloth overlaid with some food and passed to Sarah, who hardly dares breathe as she walks from Elm Hill to Conesford, I receive quills and a knife to sharpen the nibs and a tablet of ink and a beautiful notebook Margaret and Matilda have made, the parchment ready folded and bound in soft vellum from an old legal document. I love it. I carefully copy the list of visions from the wax tablet onto the first page.

And then I stop. Silenced! Now I feel as though I have killed the visions by summarising them thus. There they are, on the page, listed. What more is there to say? But there is so much more, churning in me, pressing upon the womb of my mind and heart, longing to be born. I panic: where do I start?

At the beginning, with exactly what happened and when.

I write:

This revelation was made to a simple creature unlettered living in deadly flesh, the year of our Lord a thousand and three hundred and seventy-three, the thirteenth day of May.

And I write:

which creature desired before three gifts of God. The first was mind of his passion, the second was bodily sickness in youth at thirty years of age, the third was to have of God's gift three wounds.

The little girl comes back to me and now I smile at her and I love her for her earnestness. That child, and the woman she became, was faithful indeed, faithful to the striving to keep open the wounds of contrition and compassion and yearning. And I see that my wounded porosity has been long in the making.

And as I write, words unfold newborn into the world and the visions reveal themselves afresh and again like spring after winter; I am not writing history, though I describe as faithfully as I can what I saw; I am writing now, with more seeing and more words, my fellow Christians beside me, looking at what I write, as God directs my hand, as Jesu responds now.

And I write of my sickness and the thought I had to ask again for the first two gifts I had postponed as a child, to be ill unto death and to share the pains of Jesu's passion. I think: why did I ask for these gifts? and now I understand and I write that it was not to see God but to have feeling of compassion.

I remember what I saw and I see again and I learn more of what I see as I write. Humility and greater service, not mystical visions. Feeling of compassion, not sight of God. I was shown this:

a little thing, the quantity of a hazelnut, lying in the palm of my hand as it seemed to me, and it was as round as any ball. I looked thereon with the eye of my understanding, and thought: 'What may this be?' And it was answered generally thus: 'It is all that is made.' I marvelled how it might last, for methought it might suddenly have fallen to nought for littleness. And I was answered in my understanding: 'It lasteth and ever shall, for God loveth it. And so hath all things being by the love of God.'

This little thing that is made, it might have fallen to nought for littleness.

I remember what I saw and I see more and learn as I write. This little thing, this round earth, is so tender I would crush it by just closing my palm and now I feel the terrible power in me to do this. It comes like a shock that quickly passes. And I see that deep rest will never be found in the workings of anything that is made, but only in the love that holds it all, the unmade everlasting love that is among us.

I remember and see more and learn as I write. The love that holds this fragile sphere is strong and vital and tender and pervasive. It holds every minute particle, every movement, every need. I think of the lowest, earthiest most unholy thing: my bowels. After all my years of suffering, Sarah has found remedies for my trouble, making a potion of hellebore leaves to take when it is very bad; and ensuring a supply of dried and preserved fruits during the winter months. I have not ceased to bless her for the relief, and to be grateful for my body's efficiency. And now the understanding that came to me when I had to clear my own bowels, when I saw that the soil of my body and the soil of the earth were the same, grows deeper in my writing, for the English word for the soil of my body is *soul*, the same as the English word for my spirit. Soul, soil, spirit, earth. The same. Here on my pot, God is, because there is nowhere where God is not, and I write, smiling at the pun:

> A man goeth upright, and the soul, the waste of his body, is spared as a purse full fair. And when it is time of his necessity, it is opened and spared again full honestly. God cometh down to us, to the lowest part of our need. For he hath no despite of that he made, nor he hath no disdain to serve us at the simplest office that to our

body belongeth in kind, for love of the soul that he hath made to his own likeness.

I remember and see more and learn as I write. There is nowhere where God is not. I see God in a point, and that point is the heart of all things that are made.

See, I am God: see, I am in all things: see, I do all things: see, I never lift my hands off my works, nor ever shall, without end: see, I lead all things to the end that I ordain it to, from without-beginning, by the same might, wisdom and love that I made it with.

How should anything be amiss?

God is not absent, there is nowhere where God is not. But where then is the grief and loss and abuse and condemnation and fury and fighting and the sore earth? I write this:

I whisper: 'Where is sin?' And God answers: 'Sin is behovely, but all shall be well, and all shall be well, and all manner of thing shall be well.

'Thou shalt see that all shall be well.'

And I remember and I see more and learn as I write that sin is no thing, only there is blindness and pain. I am shown that God is never wrath, God cannot be wrath, for if God were to cease to love all that is made for one moment it would fail. I write this, and I am shown and I write that the love that encloses us and pervades every part of our being and every part of all that is made, this is the love of a mother. As a mother will suffer her child's grief and share his tears, as a mother will never cease to be patient and accepting of her child's faults, always loving no matter what the child does, so God's love is.

God is mother.

I write that holy church teaches that there are those who are damned. But I am shown no damned souls, not one, and I write this too.

I write of what I have been taught by holy church and I write of what I am shown by the visions of God and they are not the same.

But I do not loosen myself from my anchorage in holy church, even in my mind, and not in my words, even though my words cannot therefore make sense.

I remember and I see more and I learn as I write.

I hold these incompatible things that my writing shows me in my mind and heart, and I present them to God again and again, and my mind and my heart expand, ready to understand more, but I do not know what the new understanding is. I do not see it for years.

LVIII

Three summers pass as I write, Thomas, always learning, finding old words and new words in English to show the visions, seeing them afresh with the same stark power of their first showing so that they come alive again as I try to describe them, my understanding growing all the time, not knowing what words will fall from my pen and seeing the wisdom in the words unfurl into the letters and words and sentences that I write. Sometimes I write just a few words and spend the rest of my writing time in their contemplation. Sometimes the words come in a flood. My beloved, supporting, trustworthy parchmenter sisters do not stint in supplying the means to write.

But I keep stopping at the fourteenth revelation. Where the servant runs to do the lord's bidding in hasty obedience and love, and falls into a deep ditch, falling because of his love not his sin, and though he cannot see it the lord does not cease to love his servant. It bewilders me, its meaning will not come to me.

I reach this point so many times, Thomas. It is as though I am on a boat moving easily through the water, flowing through with the current, using my pen like a paddle to steer not to propel, and then

I come to an invisible barrier and my boat bumps up against it, bump, bump as the water is still flowing forwards, the water is still flowing, my words want to come but they are stopped by a solid wall. I write:

> Good lord, I see thee that thou art very truth and I know sothly that we sin grievously all day and are blameworthy; and I may neither leave the knowing of this sothe, nor do I see thee showing us any manner of blame. How may this be?

> For I know by the common teaching of holy church and by mine own feeling that the blame of our sin continually hangs upon us, from the first man into the time that we come up into heaven; then was my marvel that I saw our Lord God showing to us no more blame than if we were as clean and holy as angels in heaven . . . either it behoved me to see in God that sin was all done away, or else me behoved to see in God how he sees it.

I see no wrath in God, I see no forgiveness in God because there is nothing to forgive; I see the saved but I do not see the unsaved. And in the saved I see all people, and I see the earth and all the planets. I see this higher truth, shown without any doubt. God says,

> Sin is behovely, it is necessary to the story, but all shall be well, and all shall be well, and all manner of thing shall be well.

Holy church teaches me that many creatures shall be damned. The angels that fell out of heaven for pride, they are now fiends and they are damned. The many who have not joined the faith of holy church, the heathen, they are damned. Those who are baptised but live unchristian lives, they are damned. The Jews who did Christ to death, they are damned. All these are damned to hell without end. Holy church has taught me this. If it is true, it is impossible that all manner of things shall be well. Some manner of things. Not all.

God said:

What is unpossible to thee is possible to me.

I do not see the damned. I do not see sin. But I will not abandon holy church. My seeing is still dim, Thomas, even as I speak to you now, but I know the determination to stay anchored comes from deep within me, from a knowing that Felicia taught and still teaches me: that to abandon holy church is to abandon this fragile thing that has been placed in the palm of my hand. Friendly voices that sound reasonable tempt me to seek God elsewhere, in a place of pure undefiled beauty and truth and goodness, undisturbed by the condemnation of fanatics because God is beyond. But God still holds this fragile thing in His love and if God is here why would I not be? And I see – and I must whisper this – that holy church is part of this fragile thing that is made; she is muddled and messy and quarrelsome and abuses her power, but she also draws us together and points to God, and she shows us Jesu on a cross, and she transforms our quotidian lives with the piercing grace of the eucharist. Holy church speaks and makes real God coming to earth, His merging as Jesu with earth and with the earth's suffering, even as we and all of earth cry out in pain and grief for what we have lost, cry in fury that we have so little control over our destinies, even as we fight each other and unthinkingly foul the soil and the water and the air. I cannot abandon this in a pure oneing with God and the visions do not direct me to do so.

But nor do they resolve my dilemma, and the boat of my writing bumps against the barrier of unknowing and the paddle of my pen is stayed.

And eventually I stop writing because I do not know what to say. These are barren days stretching into months, hard months because the writing feeds my soul and now it is starved. As if to mock me, holy church has made herself a new pope in Rome even while she still has a pope in Avignon. The Lollards, whose teaching offers wisdom from which she could learn if she only had the courage to face herself, go on being spurned and spat upon and made excommunicate. Holy church to whom I am anchored does not know who she is. Her heart is divided.

I am anchored in my cell to this unkind teacher and I do not seek to separate myself and I do not take sides. I let the teaching of holy church, which I will not depart from, and the showing of God, which is true and I will not depart from, sit in me as two unmutual truths without quarrelling. I pray. Sometimes I wait quietly in unknowing, trusting that if both teachings are true then they will last, and my mind and my heart will grow to greater understanding. Sometimes I shout at God:

Where is sin, if You do not see it?

1393–1401

LIX

Felicia brings me fresh parchment and pens and firmly bids me write, even though I still do not know what to say. I am so hungry for the food that writing has given me that I simply obey her.

And Sarah brings me Gyb. A sturdy black and white stray cat that has been pawing at her door for a week, she says. I concede he can stay, for it is suggested in *The Guide for Anchoresses* and we have mice; and soon he wins my heart. After sleeping in Sarah's room each night, he jumps through my window and joins me the moment I rise and kneel for Lauds, sitting up beside me with his paws together, his tail curled around his base, his eyes like mine facing east, stock still, like a little Benedictine nun in black with a black and white wimple. He attends many of the Offices in this way, as if he knows the world he has entered and what he needs to do to be accepted. When I have visitors he wants to sit on my lap and see what I see. Sometimes he stays and his funny unthreatening presence eases the hearts of those who come. Sometimes he steps from my lap onto the window ledge and out into the garden and disappears. At first when I begin again to write he walks across my table, taking up far too much room and trying to make my pens play by pawing at them, but Sarah finds a stool I can place beside my chair on which he sits upright, watching the movement of my pen with his eyes, or curls up in a ball to sleep, nose twitching. When my fingers are cramped by the cold I can warm them on his warm body. Burying my hands in his black fur reminds me of burying my hands in my father's black hair as I rode high on his shoulders on summer evenings, inspecting our small-holding, and the memory fills me with happiness. And Gyb diverts us by his hunting methods. I see his ears suddenly prick at a sound I have not heard, and I call Sarah to watch as his eyes focus with single pointed attention on a spot in the rushes we cannot see, then he crouches, his body tense, then a writhing shiver runs through him and he pounces, paws clamping down on his prey with mercilessly unsheathed claws. He eats the bloody aftermath with revolting relish.

Gyb's animal nature grounds me and unlooses my mind and heart as I face again a strange time, not barren any more but full of unknow-ing. I am on a journey, I see now, Thomas, though at the time I feel only that I know nothing and I open myself to receive and be trans-formed by what is to come, inside my cell, deep inside me. I am very quiet.

I am inside my cell and inside myself but I am not withdrawn. I am open. Porous.

My writing is prayer. I do not know what I will write and I cannot let this trouble me, for if I worry the writing ceases. When the time comes to write, however I feel, I sit at my table. Gyb jumps onto his stool beside me and I open my parchment book and sharpen my quill pen and fill it with ink and place the tip of the nib on the page and allow words to emerge. I do not know what the words will be, and in this time, Thomas, I am aware of a great listening from all those for whom I write and they are vast in number but I do not turn to them or think of them because that stays my hand too. It is as if I have to find my way through to a new place of understanding, not with my mind but with all of me, focused only on my pen, aware of this great company of listeners but finding my way alone with my pen as my guide, and I am so quiet and careful as I watch the words emerge from my pen because I do not know what they will say and they will only say these new seeings if I do not interrupt them with any idea, any idea at all, Thomas, of what they ought to say or for whom they say it.

And as with my writing, so with my private prayer before the image of my beloved brother and mother, Jesu. My unknowing is deeper than it has ever been. No matter how I feel, when the time in the day comes to pray, I wash my face and smooth my clothes and kneel, and slow down my breath, and speak the *Pater Noster* at a slow pace accompanied by Gyb's deep purring. Slowly, prayer – open, deep, quiet prayer – emerges in me and I can bring the names of those for whom I pray into the great warmth of God's Presence and give them into that comfort and beauty. And when I have prayed their names I fall into silence and sometimes it is a beseeching silence, a longing, an emptiness with nothing to fill it, and sometimes it is full and there is no need for trust or faith or any movement at all because I am not even aware of my own place, there is only God, and all is well.

And my counselling takes the same more deeply unknowing form. When I open the curtain of my cell and the eyes and heart of me to the person seeking me, I know nothing at all and I do not speak. I only listen. Those who come learn that they will not be taught by me, but by the movement of God in their own hearts. And that they are safe to speak freely when they are with me. Even the Bishop's spies cannot provoke words from me at this time.

As the world is cramping itself in distorted fear of persecution, I am learning a new language. It is for all people and I cannot jeopardise the learning with fear that the words will be wrong and my thinking heretical. I follow the thread of the writing on the page, the stillness in prayer, the words I hear from my visitors, and the invisible barrier stopping my boat opens, just a little, just enough to move through carefully, carefully, and now I am in a narrow river and it is turbulent all around me and the thread I am following is leading me through the turbulence that I feel but do not heed, so closely am I attending to the thread that is guiding me through.

It is a time of great unknowing, of trusting, of care, of deep quiet, open to all that surrounds me: fear of persecution, and grief still at the great loss of the pestilence, and anger at the injustice of those who wield power, and terror at what is yet to come, and I am not separated by a hard membrane any more but porous to it and I know nothing. Now I can see, Thomas, that by grace my anchorhold is a tiny, steady light in the heart of a great swirling troublous darkness, and it draws people to it who are perhaps strengthened, but I myself know nothing save to follow this thread. Not for myself. For all.

LX

I make all things well.

How?

Look again at the lord and the servant. Look at every detail. Learn.

I watch the words emerge from my pen and the fourteenth revelation comes to life once more. The lord is seated and the servant stands before him. The lord is seated not like Bishop Henry high up above us all but on the ground, the earth; and the earth is dry, barren. The face of the lord and the face of the servant are shining. They are in love with each other, this lordly squatter and the eager young man. And the lord speaks, though still I cannot hear what he is saying, and the servant gathers himself on the instant of hearing his words and turns to do his bidding, and runs in great haste, and trips, and falls into a deep ditch. As I had seen before. I look back up at the lord, who now is high up, high up above the fallen young man, like the Bishop in the cathedral but only because the man has fallen so deeply, and I can see the lord's face, which is entirely towards the young man and it is shining still with unchanged love and yearning. The lord has not moved from his place on the barren earth. And I look back at the young man and he is groaning, bruised, unable to move, and he has fallen so his face is away from the lord and he cannot see the look of love on his lord's face and he is completely alone, body crumpled and in pain and abandoned, unloved, deep in the ravine whence he had fallen only because he longed to serve his lord. Only because he longed to serve his lord. Not because he sinned.

Look again, Julian.

I look back at the lord still sitting on the earth but so high above the servant and now I can see into his heart and I feel a great joy, a magnificent joy, but a waiting joy. It is the suppressed excitement of a father who knows that however much his sick child is suffering she will be healed and made a thousand times better when she emerges from her pain. A thousand times better. The pain will bring her there. And so he weeps for her pain but he is also brimming with anticipated joy. He is weeping, and yet his heart is bursting with a joy that fills the heavens as he regards his fallen servant. His pity and his joy flow from him and enwrap the servant, holding him in love even as he lies prone in pain.

And I look back at the poor servant, lying in the mud, moaning and weeping, unable to move, his face in the mud, turned away from his lord, utterly unknowing. I look into him. He has not sinned. He was just in a hurry to obey.

Look more closely, Julian.

And now I can see into the servant's heart and I see that his love of his lord is unchanged. His will to serve his lord is unchanged. But he is stunned: he does not know himself. And he cannot see his lord.

Is *this* sin?

Servant in the mud, who *are* you?

Look more closely, Julian.

And now the servant is before the lord once more, ready to start and do his will. The pageant is replayed. And I see that the characters do not resemble those I saw in the pageants of my youth as much as I had thought in my first seeing of this strange parable. The servant is wearing the clothes of a worker, a kirtle to just below his knee, undyed linen, muddy and crusty with sweat, as though he has been labouring for a long time.

Are you Adam? Are you all of us? Why are you standing so close to the lord in your filthy rags?

The lord sits serenely on the barren earth. His rich robes are blue, fulsome and flowing, layer upon layer, fold upon fold encompassing the lord and falling from his shoulders to the ground, billowing all around him. His face is brown. His eyes are black and glowing. He radiates noble sobriety and delight.

Are you God? Why are you sitting on the barren earth? Why are you delighted?

The love ripples and flows between the lord and the servant, filling me its close observer with its indestructible power.

I look back at the servant.

Are you *only* Adam?

And the shining love that is between them is revealed as the love of a parent for a child and a child for her parent. Unbreakable. Unconditional.

You are Jesu, born of the Godhead before all ages.

And you are Adam, made by God, birthing all humanity.

One.

And now I can hear the words of the loving lord to his beloved Jesu and Adam, the words that Jesu-Adam starts and runs to obey.

I hunger.

And Jesu-Adam goes to bring food for his lord, but the food has to be grown from the barren earth and now I see the son-servant on his knees with his hands in the earth, gently dislodging the hard soil, crumbling it in his fingers so the moisture comes, softening and serving the earth on his knees with no aid but his own body to bring its fertility back to life to make it fruitful again and the fruit is the food of God, the only food that will nourish Him. And the work is hard and long and concentrated and vital because without the fruit of the earth God starves.

And like a second player but it is the same young man, Adam-Jesu gardens the earth but his hands are not gentle, they are impatient, and they do not find the moisture in the soil but seek clever quick ways of making the soil do his bidding so it produces fruit, but the fruit is forced and has no sweetness and the earth is suffering from being compelled to give birth to untimely fruit, too much of it, like a woman's body worn and diseased by too much childbirth. And now Adam-Jesu seems to have forgotten the hunger of the lord and is intent only upon production and more production, exhausting himself, exhausting the soil, until he falls in a swoon on his face in the mud now poisoned by his voracious haste, and he disappears under the earth.

And Jesu-Adam is gently gardening still but his calm digging does not cease and it goes deeper and deeper, his body aching and torn, his hands bleeding, till he has found the fruit for which God still hungers, Adam-Jesu himself, lying in deep darkness, full of shame at his foolish well-intended greed, helpless to amend, and Jesu-Adam brings him forth, up into the light, and Adam-Jesu is holding the hands of all humanity, all of us, I know not how, in our muddled mistaken lost helplessness, leading thousands upon thousands upon thousands of souls till all the souls of the world are released into the light, their pain ended, their sight restored and they gaze upon the loving lord whose love has never ceased only Adam-Jesu could not see it.

And Jesu-Adam has felt all that pain, that shame; has gone to its source and been torn and wounded by it until he has found Adam-Jesu and brought him into light.

And now the gardening begins again, taken up by all humanity in imitation of Jesu-Adam's gentle, unhurried tending, and the lord eats of the unforced fruit and at last he is satisfied.

And Jesu-Adam-Jesu is with him, and his beloved mother Mary is with him, and all the thousands upon thousands of souls are with him, none excluded, as if they are one soul, and the rejoicing is beyond all that I can say.

I . . . marvel.

Sin is behovely, but all shall be well, and all shall be well, and all manner of thing shall be well.

All not some. All.

LXI

I put down my pen, and time and space are compressed and stretched out. My attention expands through the window on my right into the fearful church and through the window on my left to the fearful world, out, out, within and through all the fighting and fractiousness and grief and terrible turning upon each other to distract from the pain of loss, and I feel the love that never abates flow and flow and fill all the spaces and be fierce and tender and in pain and unconditional and funny, and it is the most real thing, the love that sits, always, in the harsh clash of fearful lost and blinded human souls who will be tempested but will not be overcome.

Because the love will endure, because we are Adam but we are also Jesu and in us is the unbreakable will to goodness and the flowing unstoppable love and *all shall be well.*

Oh Thomas, your listening is like a thirst and it is drawing these words, so many words, from me. Again the visions live, again there is more to see. It will always be so. Love will never cease to be performed.

LXII

L ate in the year that my writing resumes, my confessor Roger
Reed dies. He has become a dear friend and guide, and I miss
him; his thoughtful legacy of money is no recompense for his
company. You are ready, Thomas, to advise on a new confessor before
the Bishop and Father Robert produce one whom I cannot trust. You
send me Hugh, a priest from neighbouring Austin Friars, his wiry
youthful body wrapped in the thick black robes of his order; he is
young but his grey eyes are short-sighted: unable to see at any distance
he can read the smallest letters in front of his nose. He is a scholar
and a gentle enquiring soul whom I truly believe has read everything.
His short sight seems to protect him from seeing the further-away
fears that are strangling holy church. I learn to trust him and speak
openly before him, and soon I show him my writing. He accepts my
outlandish words because to him they are not outlandish; they show
many influences and sources that he recognises, he says, and he is full
of respect for my learning. He brings me books from the Friars'
library to show me how much I seem to know without ever having
been taught. He is a wonderful companion.

*

After the fourteenth revelation opens itself more fully to me I look again at all the visions with the same eye to their detail, to precisely what I see as they present themselves, painted afresh in my mind's eye, and there is so much more to see and to understand.

And therefore to write.

Isabel, whose capacity to know what is going on never ceases to amaze me, sends money to pay for the new parchment book, a big one, with many leaves folded and stitched together, sturdy and ready for my pen. The sisters make the book and bring it to me discreetly. Sarah has become skilled at guarding my time to write, keeping visitors at bay, always warning me when Father Robert enters the church.

So there is no obstacle to beginning again. Except in me. I feel the tug of the words I have already written. I love them dearly; they are my children, Hugh has shown me how much truth they hold, and I do not want to abandon them. I try for a time to correct the old words, the ones written before the fourteenth revelation wrote itself into my deeper understanding, and I try to squeeze new sentences in between them. But there is not nearly enough space.

I have to start again; but will the new words be as truthful as the old? And how do I know that when I am halfway through this next account I will not see more and need to start again, yet again?

Confessor Hugh is reassuring. I will find much of what I have written will reappear under my pen, he says, because it is beautiful and true, only it will be expanded with my new seeing. And of course it will not be finished, of course there will be more to say and see, even as I am writing and certainly after I have come to an end of the writing. The visions are live things, says Hugh, and so am I, so there will always be more.

Thomas! There has been more as I have spoken to you now. Always more.

So I start again, and I feel a lightness of heart and relief to be free of what I had not realised had become a burden. So many times I have had to surrender the old to allow the new. The old seems so important before I let it go, so insignificant afterwards.

And the good words from before are not lost, returning to the page under my pen when needed. And each of the visions has more detail to see, and more wisdom to offer, rewarding my sacrifice of the first writing. And even as the noose tightens around the so-called heretics and the fear in the land continues to rise, I am absorbed in my task. The words are my wounds and they bleed freshly every day. And so are my prayer and my counselling – words come to me now and I speak them – open to God, open to the other, flowing, growing, welcome. I am regarded with increasing respect. I am treated as one who dispenses deep wisdom. Dame Julian, Mother Julian. I am not respectable and I am not wise, but the growing deference is some protection against Robert and the Bishop's agents. They know they would be foolish to condemn me. But they do not cease to watch me, and outside my cell persecution thrives, fed by suspicious minds and hearts. My gratitude for my cell and its protection is redoubled even as my focus on writing and prayer and counselling is redoubled.

I have to be careful. I know that I will never come to an end of seeing, but I will have to finish writing so that I can send the book into safety. Its discovery would be catastrophic, and not just for me.

Father Robert is finally moved in 1396 but my relief is short-lived, as Father William seems to have been appointed especially to spy on me. It is a year of trial. I dare not write while he is by, and he is always by. I am forced to trust that the words I have in me still will wait and be born when they can be, that they will not die inside me. And that I will be able to finish my work.

They do not die. And thankfully William is taken to spy on another parish within a year and Father Nicholas Hale is now our priest and he is a friend and a confidant, another watcher to warn if I need to put down my pen.

And in 1401, when the law makes heresy sedition and the firepit to burn Lollards is dug and the flames are lit, when the first foul stench of the burning bodies reaches my cell on the east wind, I decide to put down my pen for good. The book must leave my cell before it is discovered and stolen from me, and it must go to a place of safety.

I have written this book that will never be finished and I have handed the task of its continued revealing to my readers, even though I do not think there will be readers. Not for a long time.

Feast of the Epiphany
January 1419

EPILOGUE

By Hugh, Mother Julian's confessor

J ulian told her story to Thomas Emund in 1403 when he was staying for some weeks at the cathedral in Norwich. She did not see him again after he returned to his duties in Aylsham: he died the following year. Neither he nor Julian knew he was ailing when he was with her. But in those last months of his life he defied Julian's wish and wrote down her words, and sent them to me. He swore me to secrecy, knowing I am her confessor and I am bound by that seal of trust. I remain bound, and I will ensure this manuscript passes into safe hands before I die.

So these few pen strokes to complete her story are made with no expectation that they will be read.

True to her word, Julian did not write again after she finished her text in 1401. She burned the earlier notebooks and sent the single book of her work to the sisters on Elm Hill and they have hidden it well.

Her tormentor Bishop Henry died in 1406. But holy church continued uneasy and does so still: the Lollards are quelled but their protest rumbles on. The protest has too much merit to lose its strength and depart.

Her dear friend Isabel, whom Julian predicted would become Prioress, was so elected and remained until her death two years ago. She left Julian a healthy legacy to ensure comfort in old age, as did John, Julian's former steward and suitor. He left money to Sarah and Alice too, delighting Julian with his consideration.

Alice still lives a hermit, but I do not think she will long outlast her former mistress.

Julian wrote no more but her discernment continued unabated as she listened a lot and spoke a little to the many, many people who sought her counsel, some travelling long distances to learn from her.

She listened. And the person speaking would after a time fall into silence, and she would hold their gaze with her loving look, and the love would reflect in their faces as sweet lightness. Words failed as Love itself was set free in the encounter, melted from the ice that kept it prisoner. Their questions were not answered, nothing was resolved, life flowed on with its doubts and distresses, but I never saw a visitor leave without a lighter step and a steadier gaze directed to God.

In her last years, Julian's prayer became quieter and ever quieter. It is very simple, she said. So very simple.

She did not count the fruits of her work. And she never stopped asking questions.

*

On a clear crisp September day in 1418, we bury beloved Mother Julian. Her second and final grave, unmarked, is by the church to which she was anchored for so long, under the apple tree that Alice planted at the beginning of her sojourn.

The apples are ripe.

FINIS

The powerful, poetic book *Revelations of Divine Love*, in which a woman writes in English of visions she saw in May 1373, to a standard comparable with Geoffrey Chaucer, is the inspiration for my story. There was an anchoress called Julian of Norwich living at St Julian's Church, Conesford, until 1416, as we know from a number of legacies (see the timeline below) and it is widely believed that she is the woman who experienced the visions and wrote the book. But the extant manuscripts of *Revelations*, one a shorter version of the visions, and two a longer version, are all late, much later than the historical Julian, so we cannot be certain of this. My story, then, is a work of my imagination. But I have tried to make my guesswork plausible.

The timeline shows which characters and events are historical, and which are not. Fictional events and characters are marked in italics. Where the character is historical but the event is not, the character's name is not italicised.

TIMELINE

1340 Norwich city walls completed.

1342 Julian *is born*.

1345–8 Famine from crop failure.

1348–9 First Great Pestilence. Julian's father *dies*.

1354 The Grocers' Guild *brings its mystery play to Norwich*. There is a script of a play performed by the Grocers of Norwich in the fifteenth century; I have adapted it and brought it forward a hundred years.

1362 Wooden spire of Norman cathedral blows down in a storm. Julian *is married to Martin*.

1361–2 Second Great Pestilence.

1361–79 Thomas Whiting of Spexhall (*called Walter in my story to avoid confusion with* Thomas Emund *her confessor* and benefactor) is priest at St Julian's.

1369 Third Great Pestilence, which targets young men and children in particular. Julian's *husband Martin and daughter Lora die.*

1370 Henry le Despenser becomes Bishop of Norwich.

1373 Julian's visions take place. Thomas Emund *listens to her account of them, writes it down, and this* short text *is copied and read.*

1375 Fourth Great Pestilence. Julian's mother *dies, but not of the pestilence.*

1376 *People start coming to see* Julian, *including* Countess Isabel of Suffolk *and* Wycliffites *Adam and William.* Julian *spends time with* the lay sisters *Felicia, Berta, Matilda and Margaret* who live on Elm Hill near St Peter Hungate in Norwich. There is evidence of a community of four laywomen living like Beguines, and their fifteenth-century house still stands; I have brought them into the fourteenth century. The lay sisters are *parchmenters* (Michelle Brown has demonstrated that this was a trade open to women in the medieval period).

1377 Richard II comes to the throne (till 1399) and is an active persecutor of the proto-Protestant Wycliffites, later called Lollards.

1377 Thomas Emund *sends word that the* Abbess of the convent at Carrow, which owns St Julian's Church, *is looking for an anchorite.*

1378 Western Schism with popes in Rome and Avignon; England supports Urban VI in Rome not Clement VII in Avignon.

1379 Julian *enters the* anchorhold.

1379–96 Roger Grylle of Woodrising (*called Robert in my story to avoid confusion with* Julian's *confessor and* benefactor Roger Reed) becomes priest at St Julian's.

1380s Geoffrey Chaucer translates Boethius's *Consolation of Philosophy.*

1381 Peasants' Revolt: Wat Tyler marches on London; Johanna Ferrour takes the Tower. A great storm this year is seen as presage. Bishop Henry is active in suppressing the rebels.

1381 After the revolt, followers of Wycliffe begin to be persecuted more strongly as the protection they have enjoyed from some of the nobility evaporates.

1382 Pope Urban VI declares a crusade and chooses Bishop Henry to lead a campaign against the followers of the other Pope Clement XII in Flanders; Henry loses and is impeached for a series of failures in leadership, including not appointing a secular lord to command the expedition; he denies all charges.

1382 Authority is given to the church to detain and try heretics in its own courts.

1382 Isabel joins the Augustinian canonesses at Campsea Ashe (Campsey Ash) in Suffolk on the death of her husband William of Suffolk; Alice, Julian's maid, *decides to become a hermit herself* (there is documentary evidence of a legacy of a chalice from 'Alice, hermit'; I have made that Alice Julian's Alice); Thomas Emund *goes to* Ayslesham. The real Thomas Emund, who bequeathed money to Julian of Norwich (see below), is cited in his will as 'chantry priest of Ayslesham in Norfolk'. I have assumed that 'Ayslesham' is the modern Aylsham in north Norfolk.

1385 Bishop Henry joins Richard II's forces in attacking Scotland: a campaign that fails.

1386 onwards Bishop Henry turns his attention to suppressing the heretic followers of Wycliffe; he also interferes in the Chapter of Norwich Cathedral and generally meddles in local affairs.

1387 First official use of the term 'Lollard'. The word has various sources: from the Old Dutch 'lollen' meaning to mutter or mumble; also 'lolium', a weed, as in Jesus' parable of the wheat and the (wicked) weeds; also surname 'Lolhard', the name of two different well-known preachers of the Waldensian way, one French and known to influence lay preachers in England and burned in 1370, one Austrian, tried in 1315. Any of these might have been meant; in my story I have used the first meaning.

1388 Julian has a fresh insight into her visions fifteen years after they took place: 'I was answered in ghostly understanding, saying thus: what wouldest thou wit thy lords meaning in the thing? Wit it well, love was his meaning' (chapter 86, Long Text). She *starts writing*.

1389 Pope Urban VI is replaced by Boniface IX in Rome while Benedict XIII is still in Avignon.

1393 Julian has a further insight: 'twenty years after the time of the showing save three months I had teaching inwardly as I shall say: it longeth to thee to take heed to all the properties and the conditions that were showed in the example, though thee think it be misty and indifferent to thy sight' (chapter 51, Long Text). She *reconsiders the fourteenth revelation and starts to rewrite her text.*

1393–4 Roger Reed, rector of St Michael Coslany, Julian's *confessor*, dies and bequeaths two shillings to 'Julian anchorite'; *scholarly Hugh of Austin Friars becomes* Julian's *new confessor*.

1395 Lollards post their 'Twelve Conclusions of the Lollards' on the door of Westminster Hall, listing many of the assertions made in the Wycliffite characters in my story.

1396–7 William Tiller of Creeting is priest at St Julian's.

1397–1412 Nicholas Hales is priest at St Julian's.

1399 Bishop Henry joins forces with Richard II, appointing three vicars-general to rule the diocese in his absence. Richard is overthrown and Henry IV comes to the throne.

1400 Bishop Henry is implicated in the Epiphany Rising (an attempt by some nobles to reinstate Richard) because his nephew Thomas is involved.

1401 Law 'De Haeretico Comburendo' is passed giving power to secular authorities to burn heretics. *A pit to that end is dug near* Julian's cell *and she can smell the burning bodies*. It is widely believed that a 'Lollard Pit' was dug just outside Norwich on the far side of Bishop Bridge, a short distance from St Julian's Church, where a pub called The Lollard Pit now stands. Nicholas Watson has convinced me that the belief is unfounded; I have retained it for dramatic purposes.

1401 Julian *completes her writing and dispatches the* Long Text *into the safety of the* lay sisters on Elm Hill, *with no thought that it will be read.*

1401 Bishop Henry is tried and pardoned for being involved in the Epiphany Rising plot.

1403 Julian *tells the story of her life to* Thomas Emund *at his request.*

1404 Thomas Emund dies and bequeaths one shilling to 'Juliane anchorite apud St Juliane in Norwice'.

1406 Bishop Henry dies.

1409 The Council of Pisa elects a third pope and banishes the other two.

1412–? Edmund Coupere priest at St Julian's.

1413 or thereabouts Marjory Kempe is advised to visit 'an ankres in the same cyte whych hyte Dame Ielyan' with whom she has 'holy spechys & dalyawns'. These are Kempe's own words, written in *The Book of Marjory Kempe*, for which a contemporary (fifteenth-century) manuscript still exists.

1415 John Plumpton dies and bequeaths forty pence to 'le ankeres in ecclesia sancti Juliani de Conesford in Norwice', and twelve pence each to her serving-maid and to Alice, her former maid.

1416 Isabel, former Countess of Suffolk, dies and her will includes 'Item jeo devyse a Julian recluz a Norwich 20s'. These legacies and Margery Kempe's reference to Julian indicate that she lived into the fifteenth century, dying sometime after 1416, which would mean she lived to at least seventy-four.

1418 Julian *dies.*

1418 *Hugh, Julian's confessor, adds his epilogue to* Thomas Emund's *manuscript of* Julian's *story and keeps it in hiding, with no thought that it will be read.*

Acknowledgements

Rachel Ashley-Pain, Santha Bhattacharji, Lydia Blagden, the Brethren of the Community of the Resurrection, Michelle Brown, Gill Butterworth, Ruth Cairns, Nicky Urling Clark, Sarah Clarke, Laurence Cole, Andrew Coloquhoun, Chris Cormack, Janet Cowen, Oliver Davies, Ellen Davis, Peter Doll, Stephanie Donaldson, Hattie Ellis, Tova Friedman, Vesna Goldsworthy, Alice Graham, Helen Grant, Thalia Griffiths, George K Haggett, Sophie Hale, Rhoda Hardie, Jamie Hawkey, Tim Horgan, Michael Hunter, Maggie Jackson, the organisers of and contributors to the 2022 Oxford Julian of Norwich conference, Jer Kennelly, Jessica Lacey, Grace Lau, Tim Livesey, Ben Lobley, Andy Lyon, David Marks, Katie Marks, Michael Moor, Seán Moore, Moore's Cottage in Knockanure, Co Kerry, Eamonn Monson, Luke Penkett, Jill Purce, Rosa Rankin-Gee and my Arvon writers' retreat companions, Josie Rourke, Sarah Sands, Jane Scruton, Emily Short, Vanessa Simeoni, Nicolas Stebbing, Abigail Sudbury, Sunbeam House in Hastings, Michelle Treeve, Katherine Venn, Nicholas Watson, Vernon White, William the Cat, Rowan Williams, Laura Wilson, Alfreda Zanenga.